WHACKED IN WHITECHAPEL

CASSIE COBURN MYSTERY #3

SAMANTHA SILVER

Cover design by ebooklaunch.com

❀ Created with Vellum

I am at the hospital. Come now.

I stared at the text I'd just received from Violet Despuis. She was the best detective I knew–and if you asked her she'd say the best detective in the world, which might even be accurate–but it meant she dealt with a *lot* of criminals. And I worried that unfortunately, this time, one might have gotten the best of her.

The Royal London? I texted back as I grabbed my jacket and purse off the stand in the hall and made my way toward the door, promising Biscuit, my little orange cat, that I'd be back later. This was an emergency. I hoped Violet was ok; the fact that she could still text was a good sign, at least.

Violet's reply confirmed that was where she was, and two minutes later I was throwing myself into a cab and barking orders at the cabbie like it was a life or death situation. The fact of the matter was, for all I knew, that was what it was.

Had Violet been shot? Maybe she'd been beaten half to death. When could it have happened? I hadn't seen her since the previous day. Oh God, what if she'd been attacked last night and no one found her until this morning? My heart seized with panic and apprehension as the cabbie pulled up to the main hospital in London. The Royal London Hospital was in Whitechapel, a gorgeous, modern building lined with multi-colored glass panels. I didn't notice any of that right now, though. I paid the cabbie and practically ran into the Accident and Emergency room. I made my way to the counter.

"I'm here to see Violet Despuis," I said to the nurse behind the desk, who raised an eyebrow at me. She was composed, but the red puffiness of her eyes gave away that she'd been crying recently. Still, I was so worried about Violet that I didn't give it another thought.

"I'm afraid you're in the wrong part of the hospital," she told me. "This is Accident and Emergency; you'll find Violet Despuis in ward 13F."

I made my way to the elevator, glancing at a map of the hospital. Ward 13F: Infection, Regional HIV and Respiratory Medicine. My chest tightened. Had Violet had a health scare? The elevator felt like it was taking forever, and when it finally arrived I mashed the button for the thirteenth floor. I watched as the numbers on the screen changed slowly–far too slowly for my liking. Ten, eleven, twelve. Finally, it reached the thirteenth floor and stopped.

As soon the doors opened I was met by a London police constable, wearing the regular uniform of a white short-sleeved shirt and a cargo vest with radio, labels and pockets. She was young, early twenties, with short brown hair and a hard mouth.

"I'm sorry madam," she told me, holding out her hand, palm facing toward me, stopping me from leaving the elevator. "This floor is closed."

"Violet told me to meet her here," I argued, trying to look around the woman. Why was the whole floor closed?

"Violet Despuis?" the woman asked suspiciously, and I nodded.

"Yeah. She told me to meet her here."

"Come with me," the woman ordered, spinning around on her heel and making her way into the ward. It looked like every single other hospital ward I'd ever been in, including the one on the fourth floor that I'd visited in the past. With beige walls, sterile tile floors and medical equipment lining the walls, this could have been any hospital on earth. I followed the woman past an unmanned reception desk, past the beds in ward 13F, and to a room at the back of the hall. The closer we got, the more the police presence increased. What on earth was going on?

"Miss Despuis?" the constable asked. "I have a woman here to see you."

"If she has dark hair and looks panicked, then send her in," replied a voice with a strong French accent.

I rolled my eyes as I pushed past and entered the room Violet was in. It was small; just a supply closet. Toilet paper rolls and cleaning fluid were stacked on shelves. "Are you all right?" I asked her, looking her up and down. Her long, dark brown hair was tied back in a ponytail, and she was wearing a mid-thigh length plaid skirt with matching socks and a black off-the-shoulder t-shirt that read *Paris>London.*

"Well, I am fine," she replied. "This woman, on the other hand, is not." Violet motioned to the floor, where a body lay. The victim was female, and going by the fact that the back of her blonde head had been caved in, I assumed blunt force trauma was the cause of death. Still, I wasn't worried about her right now.

"So you're not injured?" I asked Violet.

"No, of course I am not," Violet replied.

"Then why on *earth* would you send me a text telling me to come to the hospital now?" I asked, my confusion turning to outrage. I'd been *worried*.

"Well, because I am at the hospital, and I wanted you to come now."

"I was worried you'd been shot!" I practically shouted at her, noticing that every face in the room was now turned toward me. "So maybe next time you could, you know, be a little bit more detailed when you ask someone to go to the hospital to see them immediately."

A small smile crept up Violet's face. "I am glad you care, Cassie. I will be honest with you, because you care. I phrased the text the way I did as a test; I wanted to see how long it would take someone to get from Kensington to the hospital if they believed it was an emergency. It took you thirty-eight minutes. I am impressed."

I pinched the bridge of my nose and closed my eyes. "Do they have a mental ward in this hospital?" I asked. "Because I'm pretty much ready to have you committed myself. And they'll listen to me. I'm a doctor."

Ok, so I was *almost* a doctor. A few months before I was supposed to finish my residency and finally graduate from Stanford Medical School, I was hit by a car which derailed not only my degree, but also my life. Finding myself falling into a depression, I packed up my things on a whim and moved to London, where I met Violet. Sometimes I felt like medical school was a piece of cake compared to trying to figure that woman out.

"I am aware of your medical training; that is why I called for you to come."

"It looks like someone bashed her in the head," I replied.

"Yes, thank you *docteur*," Violet replied sarcastically, and I had to smile. I took a better look at the victim lying on the ground. She looked to be around five feet two inches tall, wearing comfortable shoes, and scrubs. She had on no makeup, but it was obvious even without it that she had been quite pretty in life. Her blue eyes stared lifelessly up toward the ceiling and her blonde, curly to the point of almost being frizzy hair was caked in blood from where she'd been hit. I looked around but couldn't obviously see any murder weapon.

"Nurse?" I asked Violet, who nodded.

"Yes. She has worked at this hospital for three years. Anita Turner."

I looked the victim up and down, then sat on my haunches and looked up at Violet. "I don't see anything weird here," I told her.

"No, I did not expect you to. In fact, it is not because of her body that I need you here. I need you because you know how they work, the hospitals. I find this case interesting, and I think that it will require some more exploration in the rest of the hospital."

"Why's that?" I asked, looking down at the victim once more. Before Violet got a chance to answer, however, a tall man dressed in a suit with a friendly face and red hair entered the room.

"Have you got anything for me yet, then?" Detective Chief Inspector Williams from the Metropolitan Police asked. He nodded at me and gave me a smile; this wasn't the first time I had joined Violet on a case which he worked.

I returned the smile as Violet answered. "It is lucky for you that you called me. There have been precisely seven members of London's 'finest' in this room since I have arrived," Violet said, using air quotes. "None of them noticed that Anita Turner was not killed in this room. She was killed elsewhere, and her body brought here. Going by the marks on the floor, I suspect her body was hidden on one of the carts used to carry towels and sheets around the *hôpital.*"

"What marks on the floor?" DCI Williams and I both asked, almost in unison, as both our heads bent down toward the ground. I looked at the floor but saw nothing, except for the boots of the other police officer who was still in the room with us.

"Those," Violet said, moving about a foot away and pointing to an absolutely tiny, dark red spot on the floor. She then pointing to another one, about two feet away. As I looked further down the hall, I noticed that in fact, almost every two feet exactly, there was another one of those marks leading to the elevator. "They are blood, most likely from the victim. A couple of drops must have got onto the wheel of the cart as the murderer was piling her into it," she said.

"But then why leave Anita Turner's body here?" DCI Williams asked.

"I suspect that whoever was responsible for the murder was well acquainted with the hospital. I have asked the people who work here. The reception desk on this floor is often left unattended. The ward 13F is not often a full one; at the moment there are only two patients in the ward. It is an easy place to leave a body, and possibly have it be left undetected for a day or so, especially if whoever killed her then replaced the toilet paper. Luckily for us, one of the resident *docteurs* required a pH testing kit, and thought that perhaps this supply cupboard may have some. It did not, but they did find us a body that had been here for just over four hours."

"She can't know how long the body's been here, she's not a doctor," one of the cops protested, and Violet shot him a dirty look.

"I am not a teacher either, and yet I can tell that you are a complete *imbécile* just from the words that come out when you open your mouth. This woman was killed just before six o'clock this morning."

"If England works like America, that means she was killed right around shift change."

Violet nodded. "Exactly. I suspect that was done on purpose. With everyone either rushing to get to work or rushing to leave work, it makes it less likely that someone would notice an errant trolley being taken somewhere it did not belong."

"So where was Anita Turner killed?" I asked.

"Ah, but I have a far more interesting question to ask," Violet replied, looking at me, her eyes flashing. "*Why did the killer feel the need to move her body?*"

I shrugged. "Give them more time to get away?"

"Perhaps. But this is a supply cupboard, it is not exactly an unused part of the hospital. I can think of at least twelve places in this hospital where I would leave a body and have it remain undiscovered for at least a week."

"Yeah, but you're not exactly a normal person," I replied.

"Perhaps not. But our killer managed to commit a murder in London's busiest hospital, move the body and have it remain undiscovered for a few hours, and it was simply chance that prevented it from being found much later. Why? Why not simply leave the body where the murder took place? The murderer obviously killed this woman in a secluded area, or there would have been someone to call the alarm. And to require a trolley to move the body, that required a lot more risk than simply shoving her into a corner. No, there is a reason why the body was moved here, and we must find it."

DCI Williams pinched the bridge of his nose. "How on earth do you propose we do that? We can't exactly shut down the whole of the biggest hospital in London while we do a search."

Violet smiled. "I would never require such a crude and inefficient method. If you follow the tracks, you will find that they lead to the lift, am I correct?"

I got up as DCI Williams, the other police officer and I all followed the tracks. Sure enough, they led straight to the elevator doors. I turned and found that Violet had followed us as well.

"Good," she said. "So now, it is a simple matter of elimination," she said, pressing the elevator's call button. A moment later the doors opened and DCI Williams, Violet and I stepped inside.

"The rest of you, stay here with the body," DCI Williams ordered as Violet pressed every single button on the panel, like an overly enthusiastic child. The elevator immediately dipped down to the twelfth floor, stopped, and the doors opened. Violet looked at the floor.

"There are no marks here," she commented, pressing the 'close doors' button. Repeating the process over and over, we continued to make our way down the elevator and toward the bottom floor. By the time we'd reached the lobby, I was convinced this wasn't going to work.

"Maybe he killed her *in* the elevator," I suggested.

"In that case we should be looking for the greatest janitor in the world," Violet replied, "as no one would be able to clean a crime scene that fast."

"I know, it was a joke," I muttered, feeling a bit of the tension in the room. However, when the elevator stopped at the first basement level, the three of us perked up. There, on the concrete floor, was another one of the marks from the cart's wheels. We'd found it!

CHAPTER 2

The three of us piled out of the elevator, and like bloodhounds attracted to a scent, we followed the path of blood marks down the hallways below the hospital. This was a purely administrative area. We passed the entrance to the morgue, and a few other doors whose names I didn't notice. After all, my focus was on the small blood marks that were going to lead us to the murder location. We made our way further down the hall until eventually we reached a large steel door.

I looked up at the door and saw a large biohazard sticker, along with a large yellow sign warning that only authorized personnel were allowed inside.

Violet tried to open the door, but, naturally, it was locked. The keypad next to the door had a red light above it.

"I'll go find someone to open this door," DCI Williams said. "After all, I'm pretty sure they'll consider us to be authorized."

"How long have you known me?" Violet asked, shooting DCI Williams an exasperated look before looking at the keypad. Less than ten seconds later, she punched in four numbers. The buzzer flashed green, and Violet pressed the handle and entered the room.

"I swear, if this were the middle ages they'd burn her alive," I heard DCI Williams mutter under his breath as the two of us followed after her. I smiled; Violet had already given me a lesson on how to get through numbered keypads a few months earlier, but it was still impressive to see her in action.

We entered what was obviously a biology lab. Large science tables lined the room, with sinks and gas taps to hook up Bunsen burners at regular intervals. Microscopes sat on some of the tables; I recognized a centrifuge as well. An eye wash station and a body wash station at the back made it obvious that dangerous chemicals were used here occasionally.

Violet made her way around one of the tables, and DCI Williams and I followed her. Violet stopped in front of one of the counters at the far end of the room. She sniffed the air carefully.

"Do you smell that?" she asked. I sniffed as well, but shook my head. It smelled like regular air to me.

From DCI Williams' reaction, I gauged that he felt the same way.

"There has been cleaner used here," Violet said. She made her way toward the cupboards, opening and closing them while muttering to herself in rapid French. Finally, she found what she was looking for, and with a triumphant cry of "Aha!" pulled out three small bottles and a box of Q-tips from one of the cupboards, making her way back to where we were.

"It is always nice to have a crime committed in a science laboratory," she explained. "This way, we do not have to wait for equipment."

"What are you doing?" I asked.

"The Kastle-Meyer test," Violet replied. I racked my brain as the name sounded familiar; in years of medical school training I must have heard the name. Finally, it came back to me.

"Oh! It's a test to see if there's blood, isn't it?"

"Yes," Violet replied, opening one of the bottles and carefully pouring one drop onto the end of a Q-tip. "I am using phenolphthalein in order to detect the presence of hemoglobin. I am first using a drop of ethanol on the cotton bud to increase the sensitivity of my test."

Violet carefully swabbed the Q-tip along the floor next to the counter, then added a drop of a second fluid onto the Q-tip, and then added a drop from the third bottle soon afterwards.

"If the sample turns pink in the next few seconds, then there is blood," Violet declared as the three of us watched on. Sure enough, only seconds after adding the third drop, the Q-tip began to turn a shade of dark pink.

"There," Violet said with a smile. "You can call your men, DCI Williams. You have your primary crime scene."

"That test isn't one hundred percent accurate though, is it?" I asked Violet. I was starting to remember more and more about it.

"No, that is correct. In fact, if the killer had simply used oxygen-based bleach to clean instead of chlorine-based, then my test would have come out negative. Also it is possible for other elements to act as catalysts for the oxygenation reaction. However, combining the result of my test with what we know, I think it is safe to assume that this is, in fact, where Anita Turner was murdered."

I nodded in agreement as I looked around the room. "You're right though. Why take the body that far away from where he murdered her? I mean, there's a ton of closets, fridges and stuff like that around here where a body could presumably be hidden for days without noticing."

Before Violet got a chance to answer, however, the door opened once more and DCI Williams returned, along with one of the constables I recognized from the ward where the body was found, and a short Asian woman along with a tall, thin man, both wearing white lab coats. The man had a hooked nose and greasy black hair. However, despite his appearance, when he finally spoke, his voice was soft and friendly.

"Hello," he said, stepping forward. "I am the head of this laboratory. Doctor Edmund Neuwirth."

"Doctor Neuwirth," Violet said, "I need to know if anything is missing from this laboratory."

"Of course," he said, nodding. The woman behind him noiselessly made her way to a cabinet, from which she took out a file which she placed on a table, and began going through the contents of the lab.

"What is it that you keep in here, in general?" Violet asked the doctor, who looked around nervously.

"This is a research area. We keep a variety of chemicals and equipment here, and also samples of a number of diseases on which we do studies."

"Excuse me, miss," Violet asked the woman, who looked up at her questioningly. "Could you please tell me what it is that is kept in this part of the room in particular?"

"Of course," the woman replied, rushing over with her file. She looked at the numbers on the corner of the doors near where Violet was standing, and then ran a finger down her list.

"The cupboards contain... extra microscopes, as

well as microscope equipment. Slides, slide holders, lenses, extra parts—"

"And the refrigerators beneath?" Violet interrupted.

The woman scanned some more, and suddenly her finger paused on a single line and her face went white.

"What is it?" I asked, the woman looking toward Doctor Neuwirth.

"It's the Ebola samples," she said in a voice so low it was almost a whisper. Violet immediately leaned down and opened one of the fridge doors in front of our crime scene. Everyone in the room seemed to all pile around as we peered into the fridge. It was completely empty.

"I'm no doctor, but even I know that can't be a good thing," DCI Williams said quietly.

"How could this have happened?" Doctor Neuwirth asked, his face blanching.

"I'll make sure it hasn't been moved elsewhere," the other woman said, quickly checking all of the other fridges. I didn't bother holding my breath. There had been samples of Ebola kept in this room, and now they were gone.

"Now we know why he didn't want us to find this crime scene," I told Violet, who nodded grimly.

"Yes. There is now, somewhere in London, a murderer with Ebola available to them." She turned to me.

"What do you know about Ebola?"

"Excuse me," Doctor Neuwirth said. "I'm the head of the microbiological research department here at Barts and The London."

"Yes, and I have read many of your published articles, Doctor Neuwirth. I find many of your findings, particularly those concerning the potential genetic factor in the choleric infection rate to be based on more conjecture than fact." The man opened his mouth to protest, but Violet put up her hand. "For goodness sake someone has stolen vials of the Ebola virus, I believe that is slightly more important than your bruised ego at the moment. Cassie, tell me everything you know about Ebola."

Luckily, when the Ebola virus had a major outbreak in Western Africa in 2014, I was already working at a hospital. We had initial extra training on the virus as soon as it was declared an epidemic, and when a Liberian man visiting Texas was diagnosed on American soil, we got even more training on the disease and how to treat it.

"It was discovered in the seventies in Central Africa, but the recent outbreak was the first actual epidemic. It's extremely contagious, but not airborne. The disease can be transmitted via direct contact with either the blood or bodily fluids of an infected person presenting with symptoms, or by contact of objects contaminated with their bodily fluids. It is also transmittable sexually. However, the lack of infrastructure, training and cultural differences made up a lot of the reason why the Ebola outbreak reached the epidemic stages in West Africa."

"Yes, there was a nurse brought back to England who had it, if I remember correctly," Violet mused. "She was cured and no one else in this country caught the disease. What about the potential for weaponization of the disease?"

I shrugged. "Unfortunately, they didn't really tell us much about that. We mostly just learned about preventing outbreaks, and treatment of infected patients."

Doctor Neuwirth cleared his throat. "*I* can help with that," he declared pompously, and I had to hide a smile. He evidently took Violet's slight against him quite personally. "It would be quite difficult, and costly, to weaponize the Ebola virus. Once patients are contained in western societies, the risk of infection reduces significantly. They could create a small bomblet, that would perhaps infect people within thirty feet of them, or infect suicide bombers who leave their infected bodily fluids on as many door handles, railings and other commonly touched public areas as possible. The virus could also be genetically modified to spread more easily, but that would be the most difficult option."

"And regardless of the outcome in terms of human lives, the panic caused by any of those options, especially the first two, would be catastrophic," Violet muttered, almost to herself. She turned to DCI Williams. "I do not believe I am over-reacting when I tell you that you are looking for terrorists."

This was definitely not good.

CHAPTER 3

e were getting ready to leave the room when Violet suddenly turned to face Doctor Neuwirth.

"Why did this hospital have vials of the virus to begin with?" she asked. "And how many were there?"

Neuwirth sighed. DCI Williams gave him a look. "If you so much as consider lying to Miss Despuis right now, I will ensure you spend time in prison for perverting the course of justice," he warned.

"We were not supposed to have it long," Doctor Neuwirth admitted. "Three, four days. There was a problem at the European Centre for Disease Prevention two days ago. A number of their refrigeration units failed, and they wanted us to store the vials for a few days while they waited for a replacement part. We have done this for them in the past, and it has never gone badly. Because our lab is locked securely, only authorized scientists are allowed access."

"So regular nursing staff should never be able to get in here?" I asked.

"Regular nursing staff should have never even known we had the virus," he replied. "There were only a handful of people who knew about this."

"I'm going to need a list of their names from you, now," DCI Williams ordered, handing the doctor a pen and his notebook. The doctor nodded and began to write.

"Send me that list when you have finished," Violet told DCI Williams. "I will be in touch."

DCI Williams nodded and I followed Violet out of the room.

"Now what do we do?"

"Now we find out how the nurse discovered there was Ebola in the hospital, and how she got into the room."

"Brianne does her studies here, maybe she knows the nurse," I offered.

"Good. Ask her if she knows who the nurse was closest to, as well." I sent Brianne a quick text–leaving out the part about Ebola virus possibly being in the hands of terrorists–and found out that she was due for a break.

"She'll meet us in the cafeteria in five minutes," I told Violet.

"Good, *parfait*," Violet said, striding off in that

direction.

My stomach grumbled with hunger, but I wasn't near famished enough to brave the food at the hospital cafeteria. I knew Violet wouldn't eat any of it either–if it wasn't organic and everything-free Violet was loathe to eat it. Instead, we found an empty table in the corner and sat in the plastic chairs. Brianne came down and met us a few minutes later.

"G'day," she said, slipping into one of the chairs next to us and throwing her head back. "What a crazy day, hey?"

Brianne was short, only a little over five feet tall, with red hair and a friendly face. She was Australian, studying for her medical degree in London. We'd become friends after meeting at Chipotle, where she worked part time.

"It certainly has. You have heard by now of the nurse who was killed, Anita Turner?" Violet asked, and Brianne nodded, her face turning somber.

"Of course. It's such a huge tragedy. That poor woman."

"Did you know her well?"

Brianne shook her head slowly. "No, I wouldn't say well. I definitely knew her. She was pretty nice, I thought."

"Who in the hospital was she closest to?"

"There were a few nurses, I think," Brianne said after a moment's thought. "I saw her and Jasmin

Kattan leaving work together a few times. I got the feeling they hung out together a fair bit."

Violet's phone suddenly buzzed on the table, and she picked it up and unlocked it. "Do you know whether Anita Turner spent time with any of these people?" Violet asked, handing Brianne the phone. She looked at the list for a few minutes, then shook her head.

"No, I don't recognize any of those names. Who are they?"

"They are the people who worked downstairs, in one of the pathology laboratories." Violet handed me the phone when Brianne gave it back to her, and I looked at the list. Doctor Neuwirth had included himself, and there were seven other names below. Doctor Amelia Chu, Doctor Peter Hart, Doctor Andrew Collins, Doctor Priya Singh, Doctor Heather Brown, Doctor Rupert Jones and Doctor David Rossberg.

"Ah, well we basically never get to see those people," Brianne explained. "They generally don't spend much time up here in the regular hospital. I mean, I can't say for certain, but I can't really see how Anita would have managed to spend much time with any of them."

"Is there anything else you can tell us about Anita Turner?" Violet asked. "It is very, very important."

Brianne thought for a moment. "You know, there is one thing. It's most likely nothing, but maybe a week ago I had to go to the nurses' station to get something, and saw Anita there. I thought she was crying. I asked her what was wrong, and she said nothing. I didn't really think any more of it."

"One week ago," Violet said. "Do you remember the exact date?"

Brianne squeezed her eyes shut as she tried to remember. "Yes," she replied finally. "It had to have been the twelfth, last Monday. It was the day I tried to take blood from a twelve-year-old with a phobia of needles and he vomited all over me. Why, is it important?"

I burst out laughing at Brianne's story, but Violet simply nodded slowly. "I do not yet know what is important and what is not. At this point, I am simply gathering as much data as possible. It would be dangerous to decide what is important and what is not this early in an investigation. Thank you Brianne, you have been very helpful."

Brianne nodded and got up. "I'll text you later," she told me before waving goodbye and heading back to the wards.

I looked at Violet. "So now we find Jasmin Kattan?" I asked. She nodded in reply.

"Yes. Yes, that is our next stop. There are eight people on the list that DCI Williams was given by Doctor Neuwirth. Eight people who knew that there was Ebola in this hospital, including Doctor Neuwirth himself."

"Well that should make it pretty easy then, shouldn't it?"

Violet smiled ruefully. "If every case was always as easy as it seemed on the surface, I would have nothing to interest me. Perhaps you are correct, but also perhaps not. There is always human error to consider."

"I hope I'm right," I replied. "You can have fun trying to solve cases that just involve plain old murder, but when there's Ebola virus on the loose, I'd rather get this case over and done with as soon as possible."

Violet just smiled at me in reply.

"I hope that doesn't mean you'd rather have a good puzzle to solve than getting a biological agent off the streets," I told her, and Violet simply shrugged in reply.

"Most terrorists, they are *imbéciles*. In many cases of even successful attacks, with a few strategic changes they could have caused far more damage than they actually did. There are exceptions, of course. But I do not believe that if the intention of the Ebola thieves is to use the virus for terrorism purposes that we will fail. Regardless of the difficulty of the case, we will solve it."

"Well I just want us to solve it before we find ourselves with hundreds, or even thousands of people with diarrhea and bleeding from their eyes."

"We will. Do not worry. You have seen me work

before, and I have not failed. I will not fail this time, either."

I wished I could share Violet's unwavering confidence, but the fact of the matter was this case was no longer about finding a potential murderer. This was about stopping a potential terrorist. I'd be lying if I said I wasn't worried.

A few minutes later we were interviewing Jasmin Kattan, in the back room of the nurses' station in the pediatrics department. Her eyes were red and puffy from crying, and she played with her hands a lot, as though to distract her from the fact that she'd just learned her best friend had been killed.

"Anita was the best person, just, the best friend you could ever hope for," Jasmin told us eventually, looking at us through big brown eyes. A few errant strands of black hair had escaped her hijab.

"Was she in a relationship with anyone?" Violet asked softly.

"You know, she was," Jasmin said. "But she didn't like to talk about him. I'm afraid I don't know much about her boyfriend at all. They'd been together about six months. Really the only thing she told me was his name: Ed."

I frowned. Ed didn't match any of the names on the list we'd been given by Doctor Neuwirth of people who knew about the disease being in the hospital.

"Is there anything else you can tell me about Ed?

Please, it's important, it might help us figure out who killed Anita," Violet told her.

"I wish I could help you, but she was so secretive about him," Jasmin replied. "I have a feeling he was older than her though. I can't say for sure. Just a feeling I got. I don't even know how they met."

"What kind of person was Anita?" Violet asked next.

"Oh, she was lovely. A beautiful person, inside and out. And she was bright, too, you know. She knew so much about nursing, and medicine. She had applied to UCL Medical School here in London. She was going to become a doctor. She loved nursing, but she was so ambitious. Her parents died when she was little, and she was raised by her grandmother. She was so studious. We were in nursing school together, and she never had time for things like boys. She was always studying, always working. In some ways, I always thought she was a little bit immature. Maybe that's why I feel like her boyfriend is older than her. But oh, she was really so lovely. Whenever anyone needed a shoulder to cry on, she was there. I'm really going to miss her."

Jasmin buried her face in her hands as tears dripped down her face. I put a comforting hand on Jasmin's shoulder, and she looked up and smiled at me.

"I'm so sorry," she said. "I deal with death every

day. And yet, I never imagined that Annie..." Her voice trailed off into nothing.

"It is understandable, of course," Violet told her. "And I thank you for answering my questions. It may very well help lead us toward finding her murderer."

"Please, do contact me anytime if you need any more help," Jasmin implored. "I want you to find her killer. Anything you need. Please."

"Thank you," I told Jasmin, as Violet and I left the nurses' station.

"Where are we going now?" I asked. Violet smiled.

"Where would you go, if you were looking for the murderer?"

I thought about it for a minute. If there was one thing London had a lot more of than America, it was security cameras. Everyone in America liked to talk about how Big Brother was taking over, but trust me, they had absolutely nothing on England. I could practically guarantee that almost every inch of this hospital was covered in CCTV cameras.

"Security room," I answered, and I got an appreciative nod from Violet.

"You are improving at thinking, Cassie."

ive minutes later we were in the
security office of the hospital. Violet
was sitting casually in a plastic chair at the back of
the room while DCI Williams, who we met in the hall
on the way, and I stood in front of a giant control
center. Grant Woods, the head of security at the
hospital, joined us there as well.

"Right," Grant said as he tapped away on a touch
screen computer embedded into the panel. "What
would you like to see?"

"The inside of the pathology laboratory in the
basement, to start," DCI Williams said.

"There were no cameras in that room," Violet said
from her spot in the chair at the back, and DCI
Williams frowned.

"Just because you didn't see them didn't mean
they weren't there."

"Begging your pardon but she's right," Grant said. "There are cameras in the hallway, but there aren't any in the laboratories."

"Well, then let's see the hallway camera then," DCI said, trying to hide his annoyance. Grant nodded and typed something quickly into his computer. The large TV screen against the far wall was instantly illuminated with relatively high quality footage–it certainly wasn't high definition, but it also wasn't the grainy footage from your standard gas station camera.

"How far back would you like it set?" Grant asked.

"Five o'clock this morning. Anita Turner was killed around six, so it should be after that."

A few taps later the screen began to play. Grant pressed another button and the video began to fast forward. For about thirty seconds there was nothing, but suddenly, movement.

"There!" DCI Williams said, and Grant pressed the play button. "Move it back about two minutes."

Grant began to play the video again from where DCI Williams instructed him. The timestamp at the bottom of the screen showed it was five thirty-eight in the morning. For a few seconds, there was nothing. Then, suddenly, two people appeared on the screen. One was blonde, looking nervously around, her eyes darting from side to side. Anita Turner was obviously nervous.

The man next to her, in contrast, was as cool as a

cucumber. He was wearing a Manchester United cap, hiding his face, and he never once looked up at the camera, despite Anita Turner doing so multiple times. They walked down the hall and Anita pointed toward the door to the pathology lab. The two of them walked toward it, so that their backs were now to the camera. The man typed something into the keypad and a minute later, the door opened.

I looked back at Violet. She was shaking her head slowly, visibly annoyed. I imagined she didn't like that the man never showed his face. Anita Turner and the man walked into the pathology lab, and closed the door behind them. Grant fast forwarded the video once more. According to the time stamp, it took twenty-seven minutes to kill Anita Turner and steal the vials of Ebola. The man came out by himself, and once again, avoided the security cameras. He returned with a cart about five minutes after that, went back into the room, and another five minutes later left with the cart, presumably carrying Anita Turner's body inside of it.

When he left for the final time, Grant turned off the video and DCI Williams let out a loud sigh.

"If we're lucky he may have shown his face on one of the other cameras."

Violet shook her head. "No. He will not have done that. This was not the man's first crime; he knew very well where all the cameras were and how to avoid them."

DCI Williams ran his hand down his face. "Well then, we have nothing. We know he's a man, and that's about it."

"*You* know nothing," Violet replied. "I, on the other hand, have learned a lot about this man."

"What did you figure out?" DCI Williams asked. Every eye in the room was on Violet.

"We are looking for a white man, one hundred and eighty-three centimeters tall."

"How tall is that in feet and inches?" DCI Williams asked, taking out a notepad.

"Six feet exactly," Violet replied. "You should use the metric system, it is far superior. The man is wearing size ten shoes; however his feet are only a size nine. This is most definitely not his first crime; he is an established thief. He spent the night prior to this one at the 100 Club in Fitzrovia, and he is a smoker of cigarettes. He was in the United States military, as his father was before him. He was raised in Japan, most likely in Okinawa, and at least one of his parents is still alive."

"You're having a laugh," Grant said finally after about a full minute of silence. "Surely you're having a laugh."

I knew Violet well enough to know that she wasn't making any jokes. Nor was she making any of this up. As amazing as it all sounded, I knew that while I could only tell you the man was white with brown hair, Violet actually had deduced the occupation of the man's father.

"I assure you, Mister Woods, that I do not find murder to be a laughing matter."

"How could you possibly know all that? The man barely did anything in the video; he didn't even show his face. No one could possibly figure all that out from the video we just watched."

Violet smiled. She enjoyed showing off, and I had a feeling that was what was about to happen.

"It is obvious from the angle of the camera and where the man is standing next to the door that he is one hundred and eighty-three centimeters tall. I made sure when we were in the lab to look carefully at the height of the door frame, as I knew we would likely be seeing the man on the video. I say that he is an established thief because of how easily he broke into the room."

"Well you're not a thief, and you broke into it even faster than he did," DCI Williams said.

"Yes, and if I was a thief, your rate of successful case closure would drop dramatically," Violet replied. "I do not count myself as an average person, because I am not an average person. But Cassie, for example, would you be able to unlock that keypad?"

I felt a small tinge of annoyance at being indirectly referred to as 'average', but I put it out of my head. It was more important to catch the person who had stolen the Ebola virus. "No, I wouldn't be able to," I replied. "I mean, Violet's showed me how, so maybe with a bit of practice."

"Well that doesn't mean he's a good thief," Grant Woods said. "After all, he could have stolen the entry code from someone who had it."

"Ah, but he did not," Violet said. "There are only eight people who are authorized to work in that laboratory, and who have the access code. But this man did not use it. No, when I entered using the code, I typed in 7,8,5,4. Which is, quite frankly, a terrible code that is nowhere near secure. But this man, he typed in *, *, * to begin, which is the code to access the administrative panel for this brand of security keypad. He then entered the numbers one to four, which are the original factory default password, and then 0, 0, # to open the door. No, the man who knows the instructions to enter the administrative panel of a certain brand of security keypad is not an amateur at theft. He is very experienced."

"Well when you put it that way, it does seem quite obvious," Grant Woods said pensively, and Violet shot him a dark look.

"And yet you did not think of it yourself, what does that say about you?" Violet retorted, and Grant's face reddened.

"What about the rest of it?" DCI Williams asked. "How did you figure it out?"

"From the manner in which he walks it is obvious his shoes are a size too big. He moves slightly awkwardly, and if you look carefully you can see his foot moving inside the shoe, indicating the extra size. His hand has a stamp on it, I recognize it as the stamp used at Club 100. However, it has been scrubbed somewhat, meaning that he did not come straight from the club to here. Therefore, he was not at the club this past night, but rather the one before. The fact that he had to leave the club and re-enter, combined with the slightly visible stains on his fingers, indicate his regular use of cigarettes."

"And the Japan stuff?" I asked.

"He has obviously spent a lot of time in Japan. I would venture to say, in fact, that it was his child-hood he spent there. When he walks past the morgue door, you notice that he puts his thumb inside a closed fist every time. That is a Japanese custom normally done whenever one walks in front of a cemetery, or if a hearse drives past. Walking in front of a morgue would be considered similar. In the Japanese language, the word for thumb translates literally into 'parent-finger'. By protecting the thumb in a fist, it is said that the person is protecting their parents from death."

"So that's how you know he's spent so long there," I said, nodding.

"Yes, *exactement*. His demeanor tells me that he is a military man; however England does not have a military presence in Japan at the moment. That kind of superstition is the sort of thing one develops as a child and continues as an adult. Therefore, someone who was in the military, and spent time in Japan as a child, means that in all likelihood his father was stationed in Japan, making him American."

"Well that should narrow it down somewhat," DCI Williams said. "Thank you, Violet, as always."

"You are welcome," Violet replied. "You should focus your search on men named 'Ed' or 'Edward', on the off chance that he used his real name. That was the name of Anita Turner's boyfriend."

"Will do," DCI Williams said, jotting this new information down in his book.

Violet stood up from her chair and made her way over to the main station. She looked over the footage once more, taking photos with her phone in a few spots.

"Next time, ensure that the default password to access the administrative panel is changed as well as the main access password," Violet told Grant Woods. "It is sloppy security, that. And when security is sloppy, people far more intelligent than you take advantage."

Grant Woods' mouth bobbed up and down like a fish, not saying anything, as Violet turned on her heel and left the room, with me following after her.

"What are we doing next?" I asked. "Visiting Anita Turner's apartment? Maybe there are more hints there as to who Ed was, assuming the man in the video was Ed."

Cassie nodded. "Yes, that seems to me to be the most reasonable next step. We go to see where the victim lived."

CHAPTER 5

*a*nita Turner definitely wasn't living the high life. Her studio apartment was in a town called Brentwood, almost an hour's drive outside of London. Her apartment was just a couple blocks away from the train station, in an old brick building that had been painted white and very badly rendered, making the whole front of the façade look like it was peeling away. We took a cab, with Violet texting madly the entire time. She didn't say a single word the whole trip; whenever her fingers weren't typing at a blistering pace on her iPhone, she stared out the window, obviously lost in thought. Violet and I made our way to the front door of Anita Turner's apartment after being dropped off there, and it took Violet less than ten seconds to pick the lock. I hoped for Anita Turner's sake that this wasn't a high crime area. The interior of the apartment wasn't much better.

Anita Turner's kitchen looked as though it had come straight out of the seventies, although it was also obvious she made an effort to make it look as nice as possible. All the dishes were cleaned and put away; a gorgeous spice rack with everything labeled alphabetically sat in one corner, and her dishes and cutlery were of decent quality. The living room featured a small television, maybe twenty-seven inches, a small desk with an empty space where a laptop would go, and a bookcase filled from floor to ceiling with various volumes; mainly Shakespeare plays, Jane Austen novels, some Robert Ludlum paperbacks and books about nursing. In one corner was a daybed that evidently folded out into Anita's bed at night.

The whole place was dark; almost no natural light came through the tiny windows. However, Anita had multiple lamps set up around the place, which when turned on, gave the place a nice, warm feel. The walls were an awful off-white color that gave more of an impression of dirt than class, but Anita covered the walls with classy photos. It was obvious she didn't have a lot of money, but she made the best of what she had.

If I was completely honest, there wasn't very much here that I thought was going to help us find Ed, or whoever the man who had killed Anita Turner was. Wherever Anita Turner's computer was, it certainly wasn't here. There were only a few letters on the desk. I picked up the pile and began to read, Violet standing next to me and reading over my shoulder.

The first few letters weren't interesting at all, just bills. Anita Turner, it seemed, always paid everything on time. I wasn't surprised; going by the look of her meager possessions while earning a decent salary as a nurse, I couldn't really see her being the living-above-her-means type.

The third letter, however, was from the University College London. My heart skipped a beat as I read the words on the page.

At this time, we are unfortunately not able to accept you as a student at the University College London Medical School. We receive an enormous number of applicants from around the world each year, and are only able to accept a small fraction. We encourage you to re-apply next year...

I stopped reading at that point and looked at Violet.

"Did you notice the date on the letter?" Violet asked me, and I shook my head, looking back down at the paper. It was dated from July ninth, just a couple of days before Brianne had seen Anita Turner secretly crying.

"And yet Jasmin told us that Anita hadn't heard back yet."

"It seems that Miss Turner did not want her best

SAMANTHA SILVER

friend to know she had not been accepted to do her medical studies."

I shrugged. "I can understand that. There's so much pressure involved in the process, she was probably ashamed of not having been accepted. My bet is she was too embarrassed to tell Jasmin that she'd been rejected."

"Yes," Violet mused. "Perhaps you are correct. Well, it is too bad there is not much information here. I suspect the murderer has been here before us."

"Because of the missing laptop?"

"Yes, that is the most telling. Anita Turner did not have her laptop with her when she was killed; we saw that from the video. And her mobile phone was not on her body when she was found. Her handbag has also disappeared."

"Great," I muttered. "So there's basically no way to find out anything about who Ed might have been."

For the first time since I'd known her, Violet was at a loss. She shrugged. "I do not see anything here that might give us any immediate indication as to his identity, although I would not say we learned nothing. It seems that Anita Turner was a very private person."

"Too private," I replied. "There are vials of freaking Ebola virus out there, and who knows what this Ed guy wants to do with them!"

Violet nodded slowly. "Yes. Yes, that certainly is a good question. However, we have learned a little bit

42

more. For example, I can now say with near certainty that the man in the video, who murdered Anita Turner, is the boyfriend she was seeing."

"Wait, how could you possibly get that from anything in here?"

"Look at the bookshelf," Violet replied simply. I let my eyes glance toward it.

"There are… books on it?" Violet gave me a look of frustration. "Ok, ok," I replied, putting my hands up and looking closer. "There are a whole bunch of Shakespeare plays, Jane Austen novels, nursing school books that probably cost more than all the furniture in this apartment and some stuff by Robert Ludlum."

"Yes, and do one of these things not fit in with the others?"

"The Robert Ludlum books. They would have probably belonged to, or been for her boyfriend, Ed. But how do you know that he's the one who killed her? Jason Bourne tries to *stop* terrorist attacks."

Violet smiled. "Yes, but the man in the video had a tattoo of Icarus on his forearm."

"So?"

"So one of Ludlum's books was titled 'The Icarus Agenda'."

"I really didn't pick you as the type to be able to list off Robert Ludlum's bibliography."

"You can never know what is useful information and what is not. For example, if I had not known of

Ludlum's works, we would still not know that Ed and the murderer were the same person. We can now reasonably assume that they are. It is information, although it does not help us to find the man's current location."

Just as I let out a sigh of frustration the front door to the apartment began to open. Suddenly, a tall blond police officer entered the room.

"You! Stop right there!" he said, his hand going to the nightstick on his hip–most police officers in England weren't armed, which was really quite the change for me coming from America–and Violet laughed.

"It is all right, it is simply Violet Despuis and Cassie Coburn."

"You're both under arrest."

"Oh we are, are we?" Violet asked. "I recommend that you call DCI Williams and confirm with him whether that is a good idea."

I had to admire her confidence; I was half ready to break down in tears, half willing to see if I could jump out the window and make a break for it.

"I'm afraid I can't do that, madam. I'm taking you into custody." Violet rolled her eyes.

"Do you know why the woman who lived in this flat was murdered?" she asked the man. He looked cautiously at Violet for a moment.

"Are you admitting to the commission of a crime? Because I must inform you of your rights. You do not have to say anything but it may harm your defense if you do not mention, when questioned, something which you later rely on in court. Anything you do say may be given in evidence."

"I am not admitting to this crime, as I did not commit it. I must know, do you have to put *effort* into being *this* phenomenally stupid, or does it simply come naturally to you? The woman who lived in this flat was murdered after stealing vials of Ebola virus from a hospital in London. I am investigating on behalf of DCI Williams because the rest of the Metropolitan Police, much like you, have an IQ in the single digits, and I am the best hope this country has of preventing an Ebola epidemic."

The man simply stared at Violet for about ten seconds while he processed what she had just told him.

"Stay here, and don't touch anything," he said finally, pulling out his phone and dialing a number. When he came back into the room, he looked more apologetic.

"You can look at whatever you want," he said. "DCI Williams will be here shortly, he wanted me to tell you he's having a chat with MI5 as they discuss who is going to take lead on the case."

"Well, Cassie and I are done here. Tell DCI Williams when he arrives that we will be in touch," Violet said, and the two of us left the apartment.

"Please tell me you managed to see something

that totally escaped my mortal eyes and you know exactly where the murderer is," I told Violet as we headed back toward the cab that was to drive us back to London. Violet shook her head sadly.

"No. I know perhaps more about both Anita Turner and the man she was seeing now than I did before, but I do not know where they are."

"Great. So we're nowhere."

"We are not *nowhere*; we are in a taxi taking us back to London. And in London is a club where we know that the murderer spent time only the night before last. We will go there now, and we will hopefully discover more than we knew."

I sighed inwardly. If we couldn't find any information about the man from Anita Turner's home, what chance did we have at a club that he'd visited once a couple of days ago?

CHAPTER 6

*1*00 Club on Oxford Street had an unassuming, tiny entrance. The entire entranceway on the street was the width of two standard glass doors, topped by a stained awning that had at one point probably been bright red, but was so dirty it was almost a maroon color. The plastic sign above the awning had faded into more orange than red, but despite the shabby outward appearance I was well aware that this was still one of the most legendary clubs in all of London.

The interior looked like one of those classic music venues where you just immediately knew *things* happened. Music history happened here. The Rolling Stones played a secret warm-up gig here back in the eighties, and the Sex Pistols recorded a live album there once as well. The walls were painted bright red, with a big white '100' sign from floor to ceiling behind the stage. The room was small and cramped, and a little bit dingy looking. Lights and cables hung from the low ceilings, framed photos of times past lined the walls. It was the sort of place that made you wonder how on earth it got to be one of the most famous music venues in all of London.

The manager was at the bar, along with a woman with a sleeve of tattoos and more piercings than the crowd at a Van Halen concert. The manager was short and plump, however, the tattooed woman was tall and thin, and hung over like crazy from what I could tell.

"Excuse me," Violet asked the woman. "Were you working, the night before last?"

"I sure was, hon," the lady replied in a thick American accent.

"There was a man here," Violet told her, holding out her phone with a photo of him. "Do you recognize him?"

The woman took the phone from Violet and looked at the photo for a minute, her brows furrowed. "Yeah," she replied finally. "Yeah, he was here. I've seen him a few times, usually when we have a heavy metal band here. We had a group from Finland playing that night, he seemed to be enjoying himself."

"We should still have the camera footage from that night if you'd like to have a look," the manager told us from where he was working on some documents, and Violet and I readily agreed. The woman nodded and took us to the office at the back which was filled with papers piled so precariously on one another I made sure not to touch anything; it looked as though a gentle breeze would bring the whole thing crumbling down and bury us. It would take them weeks to dig through and find our bodies.

"Okay, here's the computer, let me open up our security program," the woman told us, clicking a few buttons on the screen and bringing up the night. "There," she said. "I've set it up for you. There's four screens there, one for each camera. Use the mouse to rewind and move forward, if you just wanna move a couple seconds at a time the back and forward arrows on the keyboard will move the footage back five seconds, and spacebar will pause it. I'll be at the front, lemme know if you need anything."

Violet sat down at the computer and I stood over her shoulder while she moved through the footage. It was very high quality, and in color. We'd gotten lucky! About ten minutes after the show started I recognized 'Ed' from his gait. I let out a cry and pointed him out to Violet, who nodded. He first appeared on the outdoor camera, entering the right side of the frame. A second later he walked into the building and a few seconds later appeared on the screen that showed the main stage area. This time his face was fully visible; he had brown hair and a small nose. His mouth was curled upwards in an almost

permanent smirk. I wasn't sure I'd call him tradition-
ally handsome, but there was something about his
face that seemed attractive somehow. He was
wearing slacks and a polo shirt with a small stain on
it. Ed walked to the bar, where he ordered a drink,
then bobbed along to the music for a while. He got
five drinks in total, and unfortunately, paid for them
in cash. At one point he went out and had a cigarette,
and I couldn't help but notice the self-satisfied smile
on Violet's lips when it happened. When the show
ended, he left once more, this time for good.

"Well that was disappointing," I said, letting out a
sigh, and Violet smiled.

"*Au contraire,* I think we now have enough information that we will be able to find him."

"Of course you do," I replied, amazed as always at
the information that Violet could glean from something so simple as watching a guy enjoy a rock
concert. "Please, share your secrets."

"Did you notice the stain?"

"Yeah, of course."

"Do you know what it is?"

"Ummm... wine?" I guessed, and Violet shook her
head.

"No, no. A stain like that, the bright pink, unnat-
ural color can only come from sweet and sour pork
from a cheap Chinese restaurant. There is no other
food on earth with that shade that I can only describe
as being radioactive."

I smiled at Violet's overdramatics. She wasn't a fan of anything remotely unhealthy; I imagined cheap Chinese food fell firmly into that category.

"Ok, so he had Chinese take-out before he came here. So what?"

"So, he obviously lives within a few blocks of this club."

"I like how you use the word 'obviously' like it's obvious to both of us and not just to you."

Violet sighed. "Look at his shirt. It is very slightly damp, and the bottom legs of his pants as well." I squinted at the screen and noticed she was right.

"Wow, that's *very* light rain indeed."

"*Exactement*. That night it rained, but it was reasonably light. You will notice that he did not bring an umbrella. There are two underground stations nearby, but it was raining heavily enough that had he walked from there he would have been wetter than that."

"What about the bus?" I offered, but Violet shook her head.

"Did you see a bus pass on the street just before he entered? No, you did not. And it is the same thing with the taxi. A taxi would have parked directly in front of the camera to drop him off. No, he came on foot, and he must live approximately, I would say, one hundred meters of the 100 Club in order to have got as wet as he did."

I threw up my hands. "There have to be like, a

thousand people that live within a hundred meters of here."

"Yes," Violet nodded, "But a lot less than that bought cheap Chinese food the other night."

"Ohhhh," I said, realizing where Violet was going with this. "You think he bought the Chinese from somewhere near here."

"I do," Violet said. "Ed is not a young man. He would appear to be in his late thirties, perhaps early forties. He is not of the demographic to use a delivery service such as Deliveroo or JustEat; he would likely have found a Chinese food place near to his home that he enjoyed, and visited it regularly."

"So now we just have to visit all the Chinese food places around here. There can only be what, like a hundred of them?"

"Well, it is not so difficult as that. We are on the border right now of two neighborhoods, Fitzrovia and Soho, that are very–how do you say–posh. The Chinese restaurants around here are not the type to have sweet and sour pork on the menu. They are very much more into the *gastronomie* around here. In fact, I can think of only two restaurants two hundred meters around here that would make the type of Chinese food that Ed had two nights ago."

"Maybe there are more that you just don't know about," I offered.

"There are not," Violet said matter of factly, and I

smiled to myself. It looked as though our next stop was going to be much more delicious than this one!

By the time we reached Red Dragon Kitchen, a hole-in-the-wall tucked away in the tiny basement underneath an old bookstore, my stomach was really grumbling. After all, it was nearly noon, and I'd skipped breakfast on account of thinking Violet had been in the hospital when I ran out that morning, and I'd passed on the cafeteria food.

I placed an order for the lunch special–two spring rolls, fried rice and lemon chicken–while Violet spoke to the owners.

"Does this man order from you often?" Violet asked, showing them a picture she took of Ed from the 100 Club security footage. Unlike the hospital photos, this one showed his face very clearly. The woman, around fifty years old and from China, shook her head.

"No, I don't know. But my son, he does the deliveries." She shouted something into the kitchen in Mandarin and a minute later a bored looking teenager came out. His eyes immediately moved to Violet's cleavage and he perked up considerably. The mom said something to him again and he held out his hand for the phone, which Violet handed to him.

"This man, yes, he gets delivery. I dunno, maybe once every two weeks or so."

"Do you remember where you deliver it to?" Violet asked, her eyes gleaming.

"Yeah," the kid said slowly. "Yeah, he lives in one of the flats on Great Chapel Street. He ordered a couple nights ago, I can get you the exact address," he said, rifling through old delivery slips. A minute later, we had it: 20 Great Chapel Street, Apartment C.

"That's only about two blocks from the club," Violet said triumphantly. "We have him."

"There'll be time for self-congratulation later," I told Violet. "Right now, let's go get him, and the virus he stole." We thanked the family that owned the restaurant and went back into the street.

"I do not know why you are so concerned with Ebola," Violet told me, looking at my container of Chinese food, which was now half-empty. "The chemicals that you willingly put into your body are far worse than any virus can be."

"When eating a bowl of Chinese food has a fifty percent chance of killing me between six and sixteen days after I've eaten it, get back to me," I replied, taking a big bite of a delicious spring roll. Violet rolled her eyes, muttered something about E-coli and salmonella, and I followed her for the five minute walk to Great Chapel Street. She texted someone, presumably DCI Williams, to tell him what we'd found.

I was really, really hoping we were going to find the missing Ebola vials in that apartment, still sealed.

umber 20 Great Chapel Street housed a music store on the bottom floor, with the exterior painted a deep blue color. The apartments above weren't much to look at from the outside: the plain bricks were painted white, which somehow made the building look worse for wear than had they kept the original brick colors. The interior wasn't that much better. It was small and narrow, and Violet easily broke into the apartment C, on the top floor.

The kitchen was tiny, featuring a half-size stove, a sink with two empty beer bottles in it, a bar fridge and about a foot of counter space to work on. A miniature window in the corner gave a view of the next street over. The linoleum tiles covered the whole apartment, including the bedroom–featuring one double bed that hadn't been made–and the living room whose furniture consisted of a small desk in the corner with a laptop on it, a single sofa and a small TV. The walls had been painted an off-white color, and had absolutely zero decorations.

I didn't notice any of that when we first came in, however. No, my eyes were immediately drawn to the body of 'Ed', lying on the floor. He'd been shot in the head.

"We're not going to find the Ebola here, are we?" I asked Violet, who shook her head.

"No, I do not think we will."

Still, Violet handed me a pair of latex gloves from her purse and I put them on while she did the same, and we searched the apartment. Violet looked in the most obvious place–the fridge–while I searched the tiny bathroom and the bedroom. It was strange; Ed owned about three shirts and maybe two pairs of underwear. If I didn't know any better, I would say it seemed he didn't live here at all.

"Find anything?" I asked her when we both finished our search, and she shook her head.

"No. No virus, at any rate. The Ebola is gone."

"Great," I said, sitting on the couch and letting out a sigh while Violet went to the computer. I knew she was a good hacker; in less than a minute she'd cracked the password and was scrolling through files. The Chinese food was settling badly in my stomach, but I certainly wasn't going to let Violet know that.

She was arrogant at the best of times; I didn't want her knowing that her warning about the Chinese food being bad for me was right as well.

About ten minutes later DCI Williams and a few other police officers arrived at the apartment. When DCI Williams saw what happened to Ed, his face was grim.

"Any sign of it?" he asked, and I shook my head.

"None. We had a look, but we didn't move the body and we wore gloves."

"Good," DCI Williams said, nodding. The same officer who had almost arrested us at Anita Turner's apartment was now standing over the body.

"Are we sure he hasn't died from Ebola?" the man asked. "Shouldn't we have a hazmat team come and have a look at the body just in case?"

"Admittedly, I am not a doctor," Violet said without looking up from the screen, "But even my amateur knowledge of medicine allows me to say with confidence that a gunshot wound is not, in fact, a symptom of Ebola poisoning."

"Oh," the man said, his ears going red. I saw the other constable trying to hide a smile.

"Perhaps, Constable Carson, you should go outside and set up the police line. After all, this is a crime scene now. And please notify the investigations unit, as well as the morgue so they can send people over."

"Yes, sir," Constable Carson muttered, embarrassed, as he made his way outside.

"Can you tell anything about the murderer or the victim yet?" DCI Williams asked Violet.

"Give me a minute," she replied, making her way to the body. I watched as Violet knelt down, looked at the wound, looked at the floor, wandered around the apartment and eventually made her way back to where we were standing and stood up tall.

"The killer was likely a male, one hundred and eighty-five centimeters or so. Six foot two," she continued as DCI Williams opened his mouth to ask for the measurement in feet and inches. "The killer was invited into the home by Ed–the name he is using, by the way, is Edward Harding. That much is obvious from the markings on the floor near the front door. You can see that there are marks that come from a size ten Adidas running shoe on the tile, whereas Ed's only pair of shoes are size eight loafers. There are traces of the water the man's shoes dragged in all over the apartment, including the kitchen. If he had broken in, why would the killer bother to have a beer with the man he was about to kill, as is evidenced by the two empty bottles in the sink."

I shook my head at the things Violet was able to deduce just from looking around this sparse apartment. "That is all I can tell you about the killer. Edward Harding, on the other hand, is almost certainly not the man's real name, although it is the one he had been using for at least the previous year or so. The computer correspondence also confirms that he was seeing Anita Turner. I suspect that this is not his only residence, and that he keeps at least one other elsewhere in London. He also had an appointment with a man named Anthony Roman at an investment firm in the city three days ago at six o'clock in the evening."

I'd noticed the post-it note on the fridge with the name, date and time on it. I wondered what it meant. "Also, the murderer almost certainly took the samples of the Ebola virus. If you look inside the refrigerator, you will notice that every inch of it is full, save for a space on the middle shelf that is precisely the size of the insulated box in which Ed took the virus from the hospital."

"So you can't tell me the name of the murderer right now?" DCI Williams asked, looking slightly dejected.

"Well, I only discovered the body twenty minutes ago," Violet replied. "I am more intelligent than most people on the planet, but I am still not a miracle worker."

"That's the most humble thing I've ever heard you say," I replied.

"Give me time. I will find the killer, and I will find the vials of the virus."

"Good," DCI Williams said. "We've managed to keep it out of the press for now, as far as I know, but it won't be long before someone gets wind of what's happening, and then we're probably looking at full-out panic all over London. Already the terror alert level has been raised to critical by MI5, which means the public will be demanding answers as to why a terror threat is imminent."

"Speaking of MI5, I assume you were the winner of the penis-waving contest to determine who gets the credit when I solve this case?" Violet asked, causing DCI Williams to roll his eyes.

"If you must know, I spoke with the head of their internal terrorism department," DCI Williams replied. "When they learned that you were already on the case, he seemed less than eager to send his men out once again, after the way you embarrassed Agent Tompkins the last time."

"Oh, *le pauvre.* I suppose I hurt his feelings. Well, I did warn him that I was better than he was."

"So now the pleasure of investigating this potential terrorism threat is all mine," DCI Williams replied. "All because a friend at the Whitechapel Safer Neighborhoods Team Station needed some time off and I took over his work for a week. However, you should know that MI5 is monitoring this case very closely, and I am reporting to both my own superior and theirs."

"Ah, but it is lucky for you that you have endeavoured to solve this case," Violet replied. "When I solve this case, you will be the one receiving all of the credit for stopping a terrorist attack on British soil, regardless of the intentions of the thieves."

"Yeah, and it'll have taken five years off my life at that point," DCI Williams replied.

"Only because you do not have faith in me. I have found the thief, and the killer."

"I'll give you that, but I would have preferred it if you found him alive and in possession of the Ebola vials."

"Details, details. I solved one murder, I can certainly solve a second. Do you come with us to visit Anthony Roman? Come, it is four in the afternoon now, the London Stock Exchange closes in thirty minutes. He will surely be willing to speak with us then."

DCI Williams looked around. "I'm going to stay here until the crime scene people arrive, at least. Depending on how long that takes, I'll either meet you at the office, or talk to you later."

Violet nodded and the two of us made our way back onto the street, heading back up toward Oxford Street to hail a cab.

"Do you have any idea who might have wanted Ed Harding dead?" I asked Violet, and she shook her head.

"No, but seeing as the list of people who would

steal the Ebola virus from a murderer and kill him does not include very many people that I would *want* to see have access to the virus, I think it is safe to assume that the terror threat level being raised to critical is not a mistake."

That *definitely* didn't fill me with confidence.

CHAPTER 8

*A*nthony Roman worked in one of those huge glass towers in the city, at an investment firm called Fullerton Investments. The company directory that I looked up on the way indicated that he was an options trader, working out of an office on the forty second floor of the building. That he was above the people working in cubicles on the floor indicated to me that he was definitely not low down on the company hierarchy.

Violet and I made our way to the forty second floor, where the elevators opened onto an expansive, almost to the point of being ridiculous, lobby. It was bigger than my entire apartment, and yet apart from a few plush leather chairs along one wall, with a glass coffee table in front of them, a plant in the corner and the receptionist's desk, it was completely empty. The three walls were painted beige, with the fourth consisting of floor-to-ceiling windows overlooking the London skyscape. This was definitely a multi-million dollar view.

The two of us strode toward the receptionist.

"Hello, we are here to see Anthony Roman," Violet told the receptionist, a prim looking woman who seemed to be in her late twenties.

"Do you have an appointment?" she asked, pursing her lips.

"We do not, no," Violet replied.

"Well I'm afraid without an appointment Mr. Roman will be unable to see you."

"I'm afraid you do not understand," Violet told her, pulling out a police badge from her purse and flashing it at the woman. "This is a police investigation; I need to speak with Mister Roman now."

I tried not to stare too incredulously at the badge, and instead put on my most authoritative face.

"Of course, one moment," the woman replied with a slight look of surprise, picking up her phone and mumbling into it. A moment later she hung up, then stood up and motioned for us to follow her. "This way, please."

We followed the receptionist through a side door and down a hallway lined by offices on either side. Blue lights set a cool tone to the whole area, and the hardwood floor only added to the cold, crisp feel of the offices.

"Where the hell did you get a police badge?" I hissed at Violet as we made our way down the hall.

"I nick them from the detectives when they annoy me. I keep one on me at all times just in case of situations like this."

"You realize that's probably illegal, right?"

"Oh, very much so. But I only use the badges for good, so it is all right."

I rolled my eyes in exasperation as the receptionist stopped in front of a glass door behind which a man with black hair and eyes was furiously typing into his computer. She knocked curtly on the door twice, then opened it and let us through.

The man motioned for Violet and I to have a seat while he continued typing for a moment. His L-shaped black desk had only a couple of files and pens on it; the majority of the space was taken up by three large monitors. The other side of the room was lined with a tall bookcase filled with books on trading theory, all leather-bound volumes. The windows behind Anthony Roman looked over London. He had such an incredible view, but always sat facing away from it. The chairs Violet and I sat down in were comfortable and modern, made of leather. About two minutes after we entered, he finally looked up at us.

Anthony Roman was one of those people with a hard look to him; his face was angular, his eyes were cold and uncaring, like you'd expect from someone who worked in the cutthroat world of the stock market. His suit was obviously expensive, although next to him was an old handkerchief, probably a gift from his mother going by the feminine style, monogrammed AR, although the line in the 'R' had worn away making it look like it said AP. So he was good at his job, but he loved his mom enough to keep the memento from her. I was sure Violet could glean some sort of information from that, but I certainly couldn't. All I saw was a man with a plastered on smile that didn't reach his eyes.

"Hello, apologies. The markets have just closed and I was trying to get some last minute moves made. What can I do for two of London's finest?"

"Not a problem, thank you for seeing us," Violet replied, shaking his hand. "I'm Violet Despuis, and this is my associate, Cassie Coburn. We were wondering if you could answer for us some questions about Edward Harding."

I didn't know what kind of response I was expecting from Roman, but the one we got certainly wasn't it. "Who?" he asked, confused.

"He had an appointment with you three days ago at six pm," Violet said. Roman typed away at his computer for a minute.

"Ohhh," he replied, nodding. "Yes, of course. Edward Harding came in here for a job interview a few days ago. I need a new assistant for a few months; the old one's gone on maternity leave. Unfortunately he wasn't a great fit."

"Is there anything you can tell us about him?" Violet asked. "Anything that stood out to you about him. Anything that he mentioned about his life. Trust me, it may be *extremely* relevant to our investigation."

Anthony Roman leaned back in his chair and closed his eyes for a moment. "Well, to be honest with you, the man wasn't that memorable. He mentioned a girlfriend, I think. She worked at a hospital, maybe as a nurse. I think he mentioned that in one of his answers. What else? He uh, enjoys watching the F1 on the telly. I think that's really it for any personal information he provided. Sorry I can't be of more help."

Just then, the door opened again and DCI Williams was shown in.

"Ah, this is one of my esteemed colleagues, Detective Chief Inspector Williams," Violet said, and I noticed DCI Williams giving her a sidelong glance as he shook hands with Anthony Roman.

"Apologies for being late, I've just come from the crime scene," DCI Williams said, taking the third chair in front of Anthony Roman's desk.

"Not a problem. I was just telling these two ladies that I really didn't know Edward Harding, he had been interviewed for a job here a few days ago. He was rather unmemorable, I thought."

"Did you get the impression of there being anything strange about him at all?" DCI Williams asked, but Anthony Roman simply shook his head.

"No, nothing of the sort. Quite frankly, I thought he was a decent enough bloke looking to make himself a bit of money on the side. His CV seemed normal enough; he'd done some office work for a few different companies in the UK over the years."

"So were you going to hire him?" DCI Williams asked.

"Well, if I'm totally honest, no. I realize it's not allowed and all that, but in the interests of helping you lot out with your investigation, I'll be frank with you: I prefer my assistants to be a bit nicer to look at, if you know what I mean."

"You want a female assistant," DCI Williams said, spelling out the obvious, and Anthony Roman shrugged.

"This is such a high pressure environment, options trading. You can't blame me for wanting someone nice to look at a few times a day," Anthony Roman replied casually.

"What kind of options trading do you do?" Violet asked.

"Insurance and travel, mainly," Roman replied. "I'm specialized. It's better to know everything about one or two markets than eighty percent of all of them. I know you're not really supposed to ask, but I have to know, is Edward Harding in trouble? Because if it wasn't for his, er, his looks, I might very well have hired him."

"He isn't in any trouble anymore, I can tell you

that much," DCI Williams said. "Thank you for your time."

The three of us stood up and shook hands with Anthony Roman again–after his comment about wanting someone to ogle all day I did another button of my cardigan up before standing–and we headed back down the hall and into the elevator.

"The receptionist at the front desk seemed to be under the impression that you two were with the police," DCI Williams said as we headed back down to the ground floor.

"As you are well aware, not everyone is capable of my own skills in the art of reasoning. It is not my fault if she assumed a fact that was incorrect."

"It's funny you should say that, because she says you showed her a badge."

"Yes, they do sell those in children's toy shops. The little boys, they love to play with the fake police badges."

"Do you think I'm an idiot?" DCI Williams asked. "Wait, no, don't answer that. I don't know how you got the badges, but impersonating a member of law enforcement is a crime in this country. You need to stop doing it."

"It is all right, I only do it when I absolutely must," Violet replied, and DCI Williams rolled his eyes.

"Oh, yes, well if you *absolutely must* then that makes it all right," he replied sarcastically, and I hid a smile, mostly just trying to blend into the back of the elevator. I wanted to stay as far away from this discussion as possible.

"All right, I promise to avoid pretending to be a detective in the future."

"You'd better," DCI Williams said. "I can turn a blind eye to a lot of things, but this is not one of them."

"I will call you in the morning," Violet told the detective as we made our way out of the elevator and back onto the street. She hailed a cab and we climbed in to avoid the rain; apparently summer storms were definitely a thing in London this year.

"So what do we do now?" I asked. "I feel like it's the tenth time I've had to ask that today."

Violet smiled. "They cannot all be simple, the mysteries. But for now, there is nothing to be done. We go home, and I will do some thinking. Come to my place tomorrow morning, and we will discuss more. For now, you have a date to go on."

"Wait, how do you know about that?" I asked Violet. I hadn't told her, but Jake Edmonds, one of the pathologists at the main morgue in London, was taking me out to dinner tonight. We'd been on a few small dates here and there, mainly getting coffee, and this was our first real going-out-to-dinner bona fide date.

Violet shrugged. "It is obvious from the way you have been acting. All morning you have been idly fidgeting with your hair when we pass a mirror, and yesterday you returned home carrying a bag from Selfridges, which was too small for clothing, so was most likely filled with makeup. You are obviously going out with Jake."

"You know, some people might call what you do stalking."

"I do not stalk, I simply observe. It is not my fault that you make your habits and actions so simple to deduce."

"Fine," I told Violet as the cab pulled up in front of her house; my basement suite was only a couple houses down the street. "I'm having dinner with Jake tonight."

"I know. Have fun," Violet told me. "But do not spend the whole night with him; in the morning we will have work to do."

I opened my mouth to reply–I wasn't sure if I wanted to deny that I was going to spend the night with Jake, or tell her that spending the night with Jake would almost certainly be more fun than trying to hunt down vials of a stolen virus, but before I got the chance to Violet simply waved and headed back to her house. I shook my head, laughing to myself at the absolutely insane attitude of hers, and then immediately set about getting ready for my date.

After all, I had a man to impress.

CHAPTER 9

When I heard the knock on my door at exactly seven oh three at night I jumped about a foot. I'd been resisting the urge to check the front of the apartment every ten seconds or so, and he was finally here.

I took a deep breath and glanced at myself in the full-length mirror in the bedroom one last time before heading to the door. I was wearing my new makeup, going for a slightly muted, natural look. The green sundress I was wearing brought out the dark auburn color of my hair. I looked *good*.

I opened the door, flashing a smile at Jake as I let him into my apartment. He always looked good. Just a smidge over six feet tall, with wavy blonde hair and an easy smile that made him look like he belonged in a swimsuit ad rather than a lab coat. Right now, however, he'd dropped the lab coat in favor of slacks and a shirt that despite their loose fit couldn't quite hide the fact that the body underneath was incredibly muscular. The fact that Jake spent his days hidden down in the basement of a public mortuary was pretty much a crime to humanity, as far as I was concerned. My eyes moved to the bouquet of beautiful white and purple tulips Jake had brought me, and the smile on my face widened.

"Oh, they're gorgeous!"

"I'm glad you like them," Jake replied.

"I know I saw a vase in here the other day, let me put them in some water," I insisted as Jake made his way further into my apartment. As I rifled through the cupboards in the kitchen–I knew I'd found the vase in there somewhere just a couple days ago–Biscuit wandered out into the main living room and toward Jake, purring softly.

"Hey, little guy," Jake greeted my cat, who rubbed up against his leg contentedly.

"He has good taste in men," I told Jake as he leaned down and began to stroke Biscuit's head. Seeing the gorgeous glass vase at the back of a cabinet, I pulled it out, filled it with water and put the flowers in it. "Either that or he's hoping that by being a suck-up you'll bring him back something nice from the restaurant," I joked.

"Knowing cats, it's probably the second one," Jake replied with a smile as we headed out the door. I promised Biscuit I'd be home soon, giving him a small treat to placate him before we left.

A fifteen-minute cab ride later Jake and I were seated at one of the rustic tables at the Flat Iron restaurant in Covent Gardens. Jake offered me the choice of sitting at either the long bench against the wall or the chair on the other side, and I chose the bench. The whole place felt like a modern version of an old ironworks factory from the Industrial revolution. The exposed brick meshed beautifully with the glossy black columns, but the round, sophisticated lights and well-restored wooden walls on the other side of the room gave the place a twenty-first century, clean feel.

"So, anything interesting happen today?" Jake asked me, and I laughed.

"You have no idea."

"Uh oh. Does that mean Violet's dragged you in on one of her cases again?"

"Definitely. Have you heard the news going around that some vials of Ebola that were being stored at the Royal London were stolen this morning?"

"Of course. It's the only thing anyone could talk about at work this afternoon. Do you mean that the two of you are trying to solve it?"

"Well, we've solved part of it." I proceeded to tell Jake the whole story of the day. By the time I'd finished, we'd both ordered the Flat Iron steak, some fries for a side and a large carafe of red wine. I finished by telling Jake about the rather unhelpful visit to the banker's office and Violet getting scolded by DCI Williams for impersonating a police officer.

Jake leaned back and let out a low whistle. "You should write a book about these stories," he told me. "They're insane. You just know the paper tomorrow's going to run an article about how the vials were stolen by a man and a woman, and they'll never know the full story behind it, or what went into actually solving the case."

"Well that's one of the problems, isn't it? The case isn't solved. Sure, we know Ed Harding killed Anita Turner. But Ed Harding is also dead, and the Ebola vials were taken from his apartment." I made sure to keep my voice low; the restaurant was filling up quickly and I didn't want anyone to overhear our conversation. I realized to the casual bystander it probably looked like Jake and I were whispering sweet nothings to each other, rather than discussing an imminent terrorist attack. In a way I wished we were, but at the same time I liked that Jake was the kind of guy I could talk to about these things in a reasonable way without it being blown out of proportion.

"You're right," he answered. "That is worrying. What are the two of you doing now?"

I shrugged. "Violet is apparently going to spend the night thinking and doing whatever else it is she does, and hopefully in the morning there'll be more of a plan."

"I hope so," Jake said. "Well, I've never seen her fail yet, and I once had a body come in that had been sitting in the Thames for six weeks. She looked at it for five minutes, then told the detective on the case who to arrest for the murder."

"Ha!" I replied. "That does sound like her. What about you? Any interesting cases today?"

Jake shook his head. "No, nothing of the sort. Actually I spent most of the day getting ready for a speech I'm doing for a handful of medical school students coming by in a couple of days."

"Oh yeah?"

"They had another pathologist scheduled, but he's come down with a bad bug and rightfully doesn't want to spread it around a whole class of students, so they've asked me to fill in."

"Does that mean we get to call you Professor Edmunds now?" I joked, and Jake stuck his tongue out at me.

"That makes me sound like an old man. Nope, you can stick with Jake."

"Good, I prefer Jake anyway. What are you going to tell them?"

"I'm just going over the basics of pathology, why they might want to consider it as their line of work when they become doctors."

"Bring a centrifuge and do show-and-tell. I know

when I was back in medical school, all the guys especially *loved* the centrifuge. Telling them they get to
play with it regularly would be a huge plus."

"Well I only get to use a centrifuge occasionally,
but I get your point. It is really fun to play with.
Don't tell my boss I said that. And definitely don't tell
him that we sometimes play with the expensive
medical toys in our downtime."

I laughed. "When I was in undergrad a few of us
had managed to sneak some peas into a class and put
them in a centrifuge for about half an hour."

"Oooh, peas, I've never tried those. What
happened?" Jake asked.

"They separated into three separate layers. There
was a liquid layer, a butter-like layer, and a solid
layer."

"Interesting," Jake laughed. "Anyway, if you're not
too busy saving the country you should come if you
want to. I'd be interested in getting an honest
opinion about whether or not I'm the world's worst
promoter of pathology as a medical specialty."

"Well, I'm not going to lie, I probably can't give
you an unbiased opinion," I replied. "As far as I'm
concerned you make everything sound sexy. But I
can come and have a look for sure. Let me know
when and where, I'm sure even if we haven't solved
the case by then Violet will be able to do her thing
without me for a few hours."

"Thanks," Jake replied, shooting me a grateful

smile as the waitress came by with our steaks. "I'd appreciate it. I'll try and make cutting dead people open sound even sexier than usual, just for you."

I almost spat out the sip of red wine I'd been drinking as I held in my laugh. "You're a crazy person, you know that?"

"I do," Jake replied with a wink. "Anyway, it's not the sexiest date ever, but I figured maybe after we could grab a bite to eat or something. It's short notice, the presentation is two days away."

"Sounds good," I replied. "I guess we'll either have caught the thieves by then, or we'll be overtaken by a disease that will probably not kill an enormous number of people but certainly will spread panic and chaos all around the city."

"In which case they'll probably cancel my talk anyway," Jake joked.

"Exactly, so if it's on, I can make it."

"You're the best," Jake told me as he dug into his steak.

An hour later we left the restaurant and slowly meandered our way through Covent Garden, arm in arm, until we passed Gelatorino and decided that since it was summer we deserved a cool, late night dessert. "Oooh, I'm getting salted caramel," I announced, ordering a single scoop, while Jake went for the double—one scoop of cookies and cream, one scoop of gianduja.

"What?" he said, seeing me eyeing his bowl. "Half

the reason I work out is so I can eat as much ice cream as I want."

"You're truly a man after my own heart," I replied. "I'm just lamenting the fact that my metabolism doesn't function nearly as well as yours. But of course, calories from your bowl don't count!" I added, pouncing toward him and dipping my spoon into his bowl, grabbing a big scoop of the gianduja and eating it.

"HEY! THAT'S SO UNFAIR!" Jake said, and he chased after me as I ran down the street, giggling and shrieking like a schoolgirl. Something about Jake brought the playful side out of me. Jake caught up to me easily, wrapping his arms around me when he did.

"You can't steal a man's gelato," Jake told me, sticking his spoon in my scoop and eating it himself.

"Is that a rule, is it?" I asked.

"It is. It's the most important rule. First, no stealing gelato. Second, no cheating."

"I like your priorities," I told him as we made our way back down the streets once more. We fell into a comfortable silence, enjoying each other's company, until finally, with the night sky upon us we decided to call it a night.

"Do you want me to come back to Kensington with you?" Jake asked as he hailed me a cab.

"You're going the other way, aren't you? No, I'll be fine. Thanks though," I told him, taking him by the hand and looking deep into his gorgeous blue eyes.

"Well then I'll just have to do this here then," Jake replied, leaning down and kissing me on the lips. Electricity instantly began to course through my body. For a split second, it was like someone had taken my breath away; like time stood still. Then, almost instinctively, my body reacted as I leaned into the kiss. I pressed my body against Jake's and closed my eyes as his lips enveloped mine. I wished this moment would never end.

Just then, the cabbie that had pulled up leaned on the horn.

"You want a cab, or not?" he shouted out the window, and Jake and I pulled away from each other, both of us laughing at the awkwardness of the situation.

"I'll talk to you tomorrow," Jake said as he opened the door for me.

"Thanks," I replied. "Tonight was great."

"We'll do it again soon, hopefully with no inter-ruptions next time," he replied as he closed the door behind me.

I was positively glowing the whole way back to Euston Road.

CHAPTER 10

One thing I'd learned from being involved in solving cases with Violet Despuis was that she had no concept of either time, or personal space when she was working on a case. I got home from the date, and while I knew that she had told me to come by her place the following morning, I was equally aware that I could wake up in the middle of the night to Violet being in my apartment, telling me we had to go out and rob a bank or something in order to solve the case. So when my alarm went off at eight am the next day and I still hadn't gotten a middle-of-the-night visit from Violet, I happily pressed the snooze button and rolled over. Biscuit meowed his annoyance at me daring to try and get a little bit more comfortable, and I enjoyed the warmth of the blanket for another nine minutes before the alarm went off again and I forced myself out of bed.

After all, there was a terrorist to catch.

An hour later I had showered and blow-dried my hair, Biscuit was happily munching on his breakfast, and I grabbed my purse and headed out the door to Violet's place, wondering what the day was going to bring.

When I got to the front door of Violet's house, just a few down from my own, there was a note on the front: *Cassie, do not bother knocking, just come in.*

I shrugged and took the post-it off the door as I opened Violet's front door and made my way into her study. She was at her computer, speaking in French with a man whose face filled her computer screen.

"*Mais vous savez que je n'aurais pas dû vous donner cet information, et si on me demande, je dirais que vous mentez,*" the man said in a stern tone.

"*Bien sûr que je comprends. Vous n'avez pas à vous inquieter,*" Violet replied before cutting the connection and turning toward me.

"Ah, Cassie, good morning," she said, a wide smile spreading across her face.

"You look happy this morning," I told her, taking a seat on the small sofa that lined one side of the study. "Does that mean you know who stole the Ebola and killed Ed Harding?"

"*Mais non,* not yet. But I am happy, because thanks to the contact of mine who you have just seen who works at Interpol, I know exactly who Edward Harding really is."

"Oh yeah?" I replied, my interest piqued.

"Yes. It is nice, knowing people. Especially when they owe you. There was an event in Budapest, in which the French government was going to be quite embarrassed. I prevented it, and now there are people in that administration who owe me, including Jean-Luc, with whom I was speaking. Edward Harding is in fact, Artie Ingram," Violet announced gravely.

If Violet had been expecting me to gasp dramatically, or drop my mouth open, or have any sort of reaction to that pronouncement at all, she was severely disappointed. "Who?" I asked, and she sighed and shook her head.

"It is truly a testament to the man's invisibility that his name is not known throughout the world. Artie Ingram is one of the world's most successful thieves. However, he was never active in the United Kingdom until now. His activities were mainly centered in eastern Europe."

"And your guy at Interpol is sure it's him?"

"Yes. He is as certain as it is possible to be, at any rate. There are not many photos of Artie Ingram available publically, but with the good photos we were able to get at the 100 Club, Jean-Luc was able to determine with almost one hundred percent certainty that our man is Artie Ingram."

"But that doesn't help us," I complained. "We know who he is, but he's already dead."

"That is true, but everything is helpful," Violet told me. "After all, we now can have a better idea as to why the Ebola was stolen in the first place."

"Why's that?"

"Well Artie Ingram has never shown any sort of political affiliation or leaning. He has stolen from people on the right, and from people on the left. A person's politics does not seem to affect him in any way. He is purely a money man. If a theft can earn him a significant sum, he will commit it. If not, well he will pass."

"So for Artie to have gotten involved in the theft of the Ebola vials, there would have had to be money in it for him; he didn't necessarily want to cause a panic himself."

"*Exactement,*" Violet nodded. "Which means that we now know that either someone paid Artie to steal the virus, or, what I find to be more likely is that he discovered that the virus was to be stored at the Royal London for a few days and stole it with the intention of finding a buyer afterwards."

"And the buyer screwed him over by killing him instead of paying him, and taking the vaccine with them?"

"*Précisement.* That is the most likely scenario at the moment."

"So now all we need to do is find the person or

people Artie Ingram planned on selling the vials of Ebola to, and we'll have likely found our murderer."

"Yes, that is what we will do now. I do not believe he used his real name; I believe Ingram used the Edward Harding identity nearly all the time while in England. He likely had other identities, most of which we will not know. I spent most of the night looking through Edward Harding's computer–I took the liberty of copying his hard drive when we were at the apartment–and I think I know where we can start to look."

"Great, this is going to involve breaking laws, isn't it?" I asked. Violet's methods of solving crimes seemed to involve committing them a lot of the time.

"Not immediately, but do not fear, the day is still young. We may have to break into somewhere before the day is out!"

"Fantastic," I muttered as Violet grabbed her purse and we headed out the door.

CHAPTER 11

"Where are we going?" I asked Violet when we got into the cab.

"We are going to visit an acquaintance of mine. She is the center for criminal information in all of London. If something worth knowing has happened in this city, she knows of it. She will know that Artie Ingram was here, and she will likely be able to point us in the right direction. I was hoping that it would not come to this, that I would be able to solve the case without consulting her, but alas, it seems inevitable, and in the interests of time we will go and visit her. I will warn you, however. Lily Hunter is rather strange in her mannerisms."

"Wow, if you're warning me about someone acting funny then it must be true," I joked, and Violet laughed.

"It is true, I am practically normal compared to her."

"You know the weirdest people."

"She is not only strange, she is also dangerous. The Black Widow of England, she is known as in some circles. It had long been rumored that she murdered her husband, although there was never any evidence that his death was anything except natural. Now she spends her days dealing in information. She is a consulting criminal, for the lack of a better phrase."

"But then doesn't that mean she might be behind what happened?" I asked, and Violet frowned as she shook her head.

"No, I do not think so. I know her well, the Black Widow. This is not the sort of thing she does. It is too high profile. It has too great a chance of coming back to her. However, we will see what she knows."

Just then, the taxi stopped. I wasn't sure where I was expecting us to be. I supposed in my head I was expecting us to be at a big, looming office tower, or maybe a house worth tens of millions of pounds. I certainly wasn't expecting to see the statue of Achilles indicating that we were at one of the entrances to Hyde Park.

Violet and I walked along the small paths, separated into lanes for those walking and for those on bicycles. The day was warming up quickly; it seemed the few days of summer showers we'd been experiencing were over, as despite the fact that it was barely ten in the morning, I was already feeling a bit hot. Luckily the huge, leafy trees in the park offered substantial shade.

"I honestly didn't expect her to be here. This seems so... public... for a criminal mastermind."

"What is better?" Violet asked. "In a world where the police attempt to listen in on every conversation, where is a better place to hide than in plain view? For the Black Widow, the police can get a warrant to tap her phones, to tap her house even. But how do you tap the entirety of a public area? You cannot. You would never get a warrant for it. There are CCTV cameras in Hyde Park, yes, but they are not every-where, and the Black Widow knows exactly where to be to avoid them."

"It still seems very open," I said, looking around. There were hundreds of people and families, spread out along the lawns, having a stroll, taking their bikes out for a spin.

"What the regular people do not care about is absolutely phenomenal. She would not be here if it was not completely safe for her," Violet replied as we curled around and joined a path that ran adjacent to Serpentine Lake. We were now fully in the sun, on a wide promenade. I took my sunglasses out of my purse and put them on; Violet was already wearing her pair of mirrored lens Oakleys. About three minutes later I noticed a woman feeding the ducks.

She wasn't tossing them bread; she had a mixture that looked like oats, corn and peas. She had the confident posture of a woman who knew where she was going in this world. Her black hair was tied back in a braid that ran nearly halfway down her back, with a few loose strands floating in the slight breeze coming off the water. As we made our way toward her, a cacophony of quacking erupted as the ducks tried to find a middle ground between avoiding the strange new humans and still getting some of the food they were offered. The woman looked toward us, and a small smile crept up onto her face.

"Violet Despuis," she said in a perfect high English accent. She sounded like she could have been best friends with the queen. "It has been quite some time since I have seen you."

"And you, Lily," Violet replied. The electricity between the two of them was practically palpable.

"You got yourself a pet, how adorable," Lily Hunter said, looking toward me. I rolled my eyes in her direction. What kind of person insults someone like that? "Oooh, and she has an attitude. I like her. American, yes? And a doctor as well. I see she's recently had undiagnosed depression as well, but it's passing. That must have been your little project, was it not?"

My heart was suddenly gripped with fear. How the hell did this woman know all this stuff about me? Sure, if what Violet said was true about her knowing everything, she could have heard that Violet had a new friend from America who'd trained as a doctor. But the depression? All of that? No one knew that except a select few people in my life.

"You never did do too well in the summer months. It is ironic that the heat gets to you, what with you being the devil and all. But Cassie is not a doctor, not quite. She had trained as one, but she does not have the certificate."

"Oh, it must have been the car accident then," Lily replied. "How silly of me."

I tried not to look surprised or scared. This woman was a bully, nothing more. I wasn't going to give her what she wanted, and she would go away. That was how bullies operated. But I couldn't deny the fact that inside, I was actually worried. How the hell had this woman known so much about me? There was only one person I knew who could do that, and she was standing right next to me. Surely there couldn't be two women out there with that same weird ability.

"We are not here to discuss the changes in my life," Violet told Lily. "I need information on Artie Ingram."

"Ohhh, congratulations," Lily said, breaking into a big smile. "I really didn't know how long it was going to take you to get that far."

"You always did underestimate my skills. It is your biggest weakness."

"I do not underestimate your skills; it is simply that mine are better. You know the difficulty of determining the speed at which the normal people discover things. I have that same difficulty with you."

The two women were being so incredibly polite, but there was a tenseness there; it was obvious they had a history.

"I need to know who hired Artie Ingram to steal the Ebola virus."

"And why would I possibly tell you that?"

"Well, it is obvious that appealing to the goodness of your heart is pointless, as you do not have one."

"Usually, when a person wants something from another, they make it a point not to insult that person."

"You and I are both well aware that there is nothing 'usual' about the two of us."

"Fine," Lily said, the small smile creeping up her face once more. She was pretty, but the smile was incredibly creepy, like the sort of thing you'd expect to see in a horror movie just before someone dies. "I have some information that could possibly be useful. What do you have to offer me in return?"

Violet reached into her purse and pulled out a small box. "You can have this." She handed the box to Lily, who fingered it gently.

"Ah," she said happily, closing her eyes. "Yes, that is a nice bribe. If I am not mistaken, there is a Fabergé Egg inside of this."

"You must be really fun at Christmas," I couldn't help but say, and Lily opened one eye to look at me, then burst out laughing.

"I can see why you brought her, the American. She is funny! All right, the gift is very useful to me. I will take it. In reply, I will give you the information that you seek. There is a pizza place on Rivington Street in Shoreditch. It does not look like much, but if you go there today you will find a man who will lead you to the answers you seek. He will lead you to the people who have your vials. However, as I am certain that even the pizza shop on Rivington Street has other customers, you will need to know how to recognize him. For that, I give you the following clue: three, six, nine."

"Hold on," I said. "You can't just give us a *clue* about the guy. Violet just gave you something for the information."

"Yes, and information is only worthy to those with the intelligence to make something of it," Lily replied, and for the first time since the conversation started, her eyes flashed with anger. "Too many of the imbeciles who come to see me think that by giving me money, or power, that I should spell out for them what they want. No. The world should belong to those who can *think*. I have the luxury of being able to decide who receives what information from me. So I give it in riddles. Those who are intelligent enough, deserving enough of the information will find what they want. The others will flounder. It is nothing more than natural selection."

"Natural selection in which you play God."

"Oh, I am not *so* arrogant as that, Cassie," Lily said to me with a smile. "I am more like the pope. I dole out the information, I do not create it myself."

"That's much better," I replied, rolling my eyes. There was something about Lily that I didn't like. She was so calm and collected on the outside, but there was a hardness to her that made me uncomfortable. I could see where the name the Black Widow came from. It wasn't just her dark hair and eyes; her entire soul was dark.

"Is being the pope not the far better option? When you see a woman whose child is dying of cancer, she does not blame the pope. She blames God. And yet the pope is the supposed mouthpiece of this non-existent God. He has all of God's information, and yet takes none of the abuse or blame for God's actions."

"We did not come here for a philosophical discussion of your narcissism," Violet told Lily. "Thank you for the information. I will see you again, hopefully when you are in jail."

With that Violet turned and left, and I did the same.

"You've wished for that for a long time little sister, but it will never happen," Lily sang after us. It took all my willpower not to stop and turn around. Suddenly everything made sense. Why Lily had the same ability to deduce things as Violet.

"Little sister? You mean to tell me this Black Widow, the queen of crime in England, is your *sister*?" I asked Violet.

"You did not see it until now? I would have expected you to."

"I guess I didn't really expect a master criminal to be related to you."

"Why not? I am extremely good at what I do, but it is only my choice to play for the 'good guys,'" Violet said, using air quotes. "If I were to become a criminal, I would be very good at it. It makes sense that a close relative of mine would have chosen that path instead."

"You have the craziest family and I only know two of you."

"Everyone's family is crazy."

"My mom works as a receptionist, goes to the gym three times a week and likes to gossip with the ladies at church on the weekend. I'm an unemployed former student whose exciting Saturday nights usually involve snuggling up with my cat, a glass of wine and a good book. Your sister is a criminal mastermind that you just had to bribe with a Fabergé egg to give you information on the theft of Ebola vials. You are a consulting detective who picks and chooses which cases you want to work, you commit crimes in order to solve them, I often wake up wondering if someone's going to try to kill you today, and your closest neighbor is an old woman who I'm *sure* used to be involved in crime and watches over your house with an Uzi. I think your family takes the cake for crazy, and I don't even know what your parents do. How on earth did you even get a Fabergé egg to give your sister, anyway? Those things cost like, twenty million pounds or something, don't they?"

"It was a gift," Violet replied simply.

"Normal people don't get priceless jewellery as gifts."

"Fine. I solved a problem for a Russian diplomat in his home country a few years ago. Believe me; the solution I came up with has made him far more than twenty million pounds in profit."

"Still doesn't make you a normal person. That's a really nice thing to give away for just a bit of information, though," I told her, and Violet shrugged.

"Lily has always been quite partial to shiny things. Even as a child, she used to dress herself in our mother's jewellery. The egg means nothing to me, so it was simple to give it to her as the bribe."

"Speaking of, I guess we're going to Shoreditch?" I asked. "We have to find whoever three, six, nine is supposed to refer to."

"Yes," Violet nodded. "That is the next step indeed. We will see where this takes us."

CHAPTER 12

*L*uigi's Pizza wasn't exactly a high-class establishment. In the middle of a narrow, empty street, the store directly across from Luigi's was shuttered for good. A flickering neon sign in the window that looked like it hadn't been cleaned since I was in high school announced that the store was open, and I pushed open the door.

Of course, I wasn't exactly one to judge a place by its looks. As a student, I'd become quite accustomed to eating at places that didn't exactly look like a Michelin-starred restaurant but still served good food. One of my favorite kebab joints was literally a hole in the wall where the owners would run a spinning fan out one of the windows as an HVAC system.

When we walked in and the wafting aroma of pizza floated to my nostrils my stomach began to rumble. Violet looked around uncomfortably, and I grinned. There was nothing on this menu that was going to suit her tastes, that was for sure.

Behind the counter was a skinny looking youth of about eighteen years who looked like an extra slice of pizza or four wouldn't do him any harm, and a balding man yelling on the phone in a foreign language–maybe Hindi?–while waving his hands around. Three small tables with chairs lined the other side of the room, along with a fridge full of coke cans and bottles. Next to the counter was a long heated area displaying the pizzas on offer today; I had a choice between what looked like Hawaiian, pepperoni and mystery meat, since nothing was signed.

"What can I get you?" the young guy asked, barely able to conceal his boredom.

"I'll have a slice of pepperoni, and she'll have a Hawaiian," I replied, ignoring Violet's scowl.

The youth haphazardly tossed two slices onto a paper plate and stuck them in the oven. "Oh, and I'll grab a bottle of diet coke," I said as I took my wallet out to pay for it. The kid handed me back my change, and a moment later the pizzas as well. Violet and I sat at one of the tables across from one another as I dug into my slice. Violet just stared at hers like it was a plateful of Ebola.

"You know," I told her, "you're actually going to have to eat it eventually. I would imagine this isn't your first assignment where you've had to stake out a cheap eatery, and it would look suspicious if you didn't."

"You are enjoying this," Violet told me as she picked up her fork and looked dejectedly at the pizza. "You are enjoying the fact that I am about to put into my body a slice of pizza that is comprised almost entirely of processed food. There are only empty calories here."

"Delicious, delicious empty calories," I replied, picking up and taking a big bite of my slice. Violet took her plastic knife and fork and cut herself a small piece of her pizza, sighed, and put it in her mouth.

"Admit it, it doesn't taste that bad."

"It tastes like a shortened lifespan and increased risk of future health problems. You, as a doctor, should know that."

"Fine, we can stop at a smoothie place or whatever other hippie place is nearby after this so you can wash the slice down with something green," I teased.

"First we need to find out why Lily sent us here, however."

"Yeah, I have no idea what that three, six, nine thing refers to."

"Nor do I, not at the moment."

"Great. So we're going to be sitting here for hours."

As it turned out, however, we only had to wait around forty minutes. A few other customers had come in, but this time a tall man with a shaved head but nice jeans and shirt came in.

"Hey, Dragan," the kid greeted him. "The usual?"

"As always, thanks," Dragan replied. As he lifted his hand I noticed his forearm had a weird tattoo: it was a cross, with four sideways crowns in each quadrant to the side of it. Violet smiled at me and nodded slightly. This was obviously our guy, I just had no idea why she thought that. We got up and left as Dragan was paying, and as soon as we got back into the street Violet took two cigarettes out of her purse, lit them, and handed one to me.

"Seriously? You're complaining that you had to eat a slice of pizza and you're going to smoke?" I asked, and Violet grinned.

"No, I am not so much a hypocrite as that. I am simply going to hold it, to make it look like we are smoking. Do the same."

I leaned against the wall, tapping the unsmoked ash on the cigarette to the ground, when a minute later Dragan came back out of the pizza shop and headed toward the Old Street underground station.

"How do you know he's the one we're supposed to follow?" I asked Violet quietly as we strolled behind him, far enough that we wouldn't be noticed but close enough not to lose him.

"Dragan is a common name in Serbia, and did you see his tattoo?"

"Yeah, that cross with the weird crowns."

"That thing you call a 'cross with the weird crowns' is a Serbian national symbol. The man is Serbian. As soon as I saw him, I realized where Lily's riddle came from. It is a quote commonly attributed to Nikola Tesla, a Serbian. *If you only knew the magnificence of the three, six and nine, then you would have a key to the universe.*"

"Ohhh, so the key to the riddle was waiting for the Serbian guy to show up, and follow him."

"*Exactement.* Now we will see where he goes."

Dragan did in fact make his way to the underground station. With the influx of people, I found it a lot more difficult to keep track of him; a few times when people randomly stepped in front of me I lost track of him completely, but Violet kept a steady pace and when we finally got on a train I spotted him at the other end of the same carriage.

"You should be on that show Mantracker," I told Violet, who laughed.

"I have a lot of experience in following people. Many are much better at spotting someone following them than Dragan, we are lucky. He is an easy mark."

Our easy mark got off the train two stops later at St Pancras, and changed to the Piccadilly Line, getting off at Piccadilly Circus. Being in Central London now, it was a lot easier to follow him without the risk of him catching us; Shaftesbury Avenue was a lot busier than Rivington Street had been. He continued along there until he made his way to Rupert Street. Halfway down the first block, Dragan suddenly disappeared.

I stopped to have a look around for him, but Violet took me by the elbow. "Keep going," she said, and I did as she asked automatically.

"What's going on?" I asked.

"In the building to our left there is a small entrance. That is where he went; it is a night club."

"Are we going to go in there?" I asked as we walked past it.

"In good time, yes. However, seeing as it is barely two o'clock in the afternoon, there will be no one in the club apart from staff, and we would have no reason to be there either. We will be much better off returning at night and pretending to be patrons. So, for now, we go home and we do nothing. But make sure you have clothes that make you look like a prostitute. You will need them tonight."

I giggled at Violet's weird attempt at telling me to dress a bit sluttily as we walked back toward the tube. Since we were only a few stops away from Gloucester Road station, the stop closest to our homes, we opted to hop back onto a train rather than try and hail a cab.

I couldn't help but notice that today every headline in every paper mentioned the Ebola threat.

Ebola Virus Stolen From London Hospital
Ebola on the Loose in England!

Virus Stolen From London Hospital–Terror Alert Raised

"Do you think there will be an attack anytime soon?" I asked Violet, who shrugged.

"I do not know. I do not yet know who was behind the theft. When we know that, we will know what they plan on doing with the virus. I will say that I do not believe one would go to the risks that they went to in order to steal the vials of Ebola for absolutely nothing. So in essence, yes, I think they will use the vials. But on who, where and when I have no idea."

"Well, that wasn't reassuring at all," I said to myself as we boarded our train. I really, really hoped our visit to the club later that night would be fruitful. I was tired of seemingly chasing after ghosts on this case.

CHAPTER 13

When I got home I took Biscuit for a walk in Kensington Gardens as usual–I was all too aware that we were only steps away from Hyde Park; a road running through the middle of the green space was all that separated the two gardens. I barely noticed the people enjoying the novelty of a cat on a leash. It was partly that I'd gotten used to walking my cat around like he was a dog, but partly nerves.

Violet's sister spent her time in practically the same park that I did. This master criminal. I shivered slightly at the realization.

When we finally got home, Biscuit plonked himself down in a ray of sunshine cascading from the window into the living room, and I lay down on the couch while taking out my iPad. I started out by typing in the name Lily Hunter. I'd expected there to be a bunch of news articles about her involvement in crimes, or even just a hint that she was involved in them.

Instead, all I found were articles about Lily Hunter the widow whose husband drowned in Cyprus while they were on their honeymoon. Intrigued, I clicked on one of the articles, dated July 21st, 2006.

What was supposed to be the happiest week of a young couple's life turned into tragedy yesterday as James Hunter, 32, known for his real estate firm which he sold last year for over 600 million pounds, drowned on his honeymoon in Cyprus. His distraught bride, Lily, 23, called police from her hotel, telling them her husband went out for a swim that morning and never returned. His body was recovered by divers two hours later.

At this time the Cypriot Police do not suspect foul play.

I finished reading the article, and, fascinated, read three others. The facts all seemed to correspond in each. It seemed that after eating a light breakfast with his wife at one of the resort restaurants, James Hunter went out for a quick swim, which he did every morning. Only unlike the other mornings, he never returned. A couple of the trashier tabloids implied that perhaps his wife had something to do with his death, but no more than that. They also pointed out the age difference, and implied that perhaps Lily Hunter, *née* Despuis, had married the man for his money.

Having met the woman, I could absolutely see her murdering a man for his money. One of the articles I'd clicked on suddenly had a video appear, and my curiosity got the better of me. I pressed play.

First there was a shot of the beautiful resort, not far from Nicosia, with crystal-clear waters just off the shore. Then, the video cut to a reporter in front of the hotel who reported the basics of the case, and turned to a shot of Lily Hunter. She looked even younger than her twenty-three years, with her black hair framing her face. Her dark eyes were surrounded by red from crying as she broke down in front of the camera completely.

"Oh James! I loved him so much. And to think, I wanted to go into town. He begged me to let him have his little swim before we left. *Oh mon dieu.* What am I going to do now?"

She covered her face in her hands as a random reporter leaned over and patted her on the back. She looked so unconfident, so unlike the Lily Hunter I'd met that morning, I wondered if she was putting on a show for the cameras, or if she had simply changed quite a bit in the over ten years that had passed since her husband's death.

Eventually I decided that the mystery of Lily Hunter was going to remain a mystery for a while longer. Maybe forever. I didn't like her. To be honest, if I never had to see her again, I'd have been perfectly all right with that.

Letting out a sigh of frustration, I got up and made my way to the kitchen. Opening my fridge I was pleasantly surprised to find a bundle of grapes, which I put into a bowl as I tapped away on the counter. I was agitated, but I did know why. There was someone out there with vials of the Ebola virus, and the chances were almost zero that they had good intentions. I knew there was nothing I could do until tonight to fix it, but that still didn't stop my brain from wanting to act *now!*

In an attempt to stop myself from thinking about the virus, I looked up the speaking engagement Jake had invited me to. There was a page for it on the UCL Medical School website–Jake had texted me earlier in the day to let me know that was where the speech was happening–in one of their lecture halls.

As I read the overview I felt a pang of... something. I wasn't really quite sure what. Regret? Sadness? I'd spent most of my adult life working toward being an orthopedic surgeon. That was now completely off the table. I knew that. No matter how many motivational Facebook posts my mom tagged me in, no matter how many times I read 'fall seven times get up eight', the fact of the matter was, I had lost five percent of the function in my right hand. And that was enough that I was never going to be able to operate on anyone.

I'd accepted that fact recently. At least, I thought I'd had. I could feel the old depressive feelings coming back, threatening to drown me. Instead of wallowing in self-pity, I shoved a grape into my mouth and grabbed my phone.

Hey, you doing anything? I texted Brianne. Luckily, I got a reply a minute later.

I'm at the hospital. I'll be done in about 20 though if you want to meet up?

Definitely yes. I need to talk to you about... well, medical school stuff.

And I need to talk to you to know if the hospital's isolation ward is about to get a few hundred new patients or not.

My news on that front isn't great. Meet you at the normal place?

I'll get the first round.

I smiled as I grabbed my purse and headed toward the door, giving Biscuit a pet as I walked past the ray of sunshine in which he was lying. I needed a friend right now. A friend who knew what I'd gone through, a friend who could give me advice.

Half an hour later I walked into The White Hart, a small, classy pub where Brianne and I often found ourselves if we met up after she'd been doing her studies at the hospital.

I plopped myself down into the seat across from Brianne at a round table. There were two glasses of beer on the table, and I grabbed the one that was still full and took a big swig of it.

"So, I see your murder case is going well then?" Brianne asked, and I grinned.

"It's that obvious, huh?"

"It is. But that's not what's bothering you right now, is it?"

I shook my head no. "No. Well, yes. But also no. I just… I kind of feel like I want to *do* something, you know?"

"Is the life of leisure just not cutting it for you? You poor baby," Brianne teased, and I stuck my tongue out at her. "But seriously," she continued, "what are you considering?"

I shrugged. "I don't know. I mean, a part of me wants to go back into medicine. Being in the hospital again the other day, seeing how it worked, seeing the sounds that I'm so used to… that was such a big part of my life, you know?"

Brianne nodded. "I know what you mean."

"So a part of me wants to do that, but then I'm not sure if I'd be happy doing something other than surgery. That was my whole goal. And then remember when that house blew up in Belgravia? Around then I helped someone else I knew from the park, just a minor detective thing, but I tried to do what Violet did and it worked, and that felt good. But at the same time, I know I'm not actually *good* at what she does."

"Would you enjoy doing it though? As a living, I mean."

I thought about the question for a few minutes, then shrugged. "I don't know. I guess that's where all of my confusion right now is coming from; I don't know anything. I want to do *something* though."

"Well that's already such a huge step forward for you," Brianne said. "Up until now, you haven't wanted to do anything. Sometimes I've had to work to get you to even get out of the house for a girls' night out. This is a big step, and it's normal not to have all the answers."

I sighed. "I've always had all the answers though, and I guess that's what's frustrating me. I decided I wanted to become a doctor when I was fifteen. I knew when I was nineteen that I wanted to go into surgery, and when I was twenty-two I settled on orthopedics as my specialty. Now I'm pushing thirty and it feels like I'm a teenager again, starting over."

"You're not starting over completely, though. You have your undergrad degree; you have most of your doctor's studies done. You could always change your disciplines and you've still done a good 80 percent of the work. All you'd have to do would be a few classroom courses in whatever your new specialty would be, and then a year or two of specialized residency."

"That's true," I said. "I still don't know if I want to try something else. Jake invited me to listen in on a speech he's giving about pathology tomorrow to premed students, so I might decide I like to study germs and dead people."

Brianne laughed. "I don't really see that as being your 'thing.'"

"Me neither, to be honest."

"When you did your initial rotations, what did you like other than surgery?"

I thought back to the years that had passed. "Definitely not family medicine," I said, scrunching up my face and Brianne laughed.

"You mean you don't like looking down people's throats and telling them they have a cold?"

I laughed as a tall man who looked to be in his early thirties and was already balding slightly sat down at the table next to us with a friend, who was also tall, but significantly more muscular and better-looking. I was going to reply to Brianne when the first man started talking. He had definitely never learned the difference between 'inside voice' and 'outside voice' when he was a kid.

"So what are ya gonna have to drink, Billy?" the man boomed to his friend.

"Just a beer, mate," came the reply, and the guy made his way up toward the bar.

"Wow, that guy's mom must have enjoyed his childhood," I said to Brianne, who laughed.

"He's a creep, too, that guy. He works down in the basement, I guess because the walls down there are pretty soundproof. Has a job in one of the labs. He's always trying to hit up new nurses and medical students. He says the actual doctors are 'too old' for him," Brianne said, using air quotes.

"Sounds like a winner to me," I laughed.

"I know, right?" Suddenly I stopped.

"Wait. He always talks like that?" I asked.

"That loudly? Yeah."

"And he works in one of the labs in the basement? What's his name?"

"Rupert something? I only found out today, one of the nurses was complaining about him. Up until now I've just been calling him 'creepy basement guy'."

I leaned back against my seat and groaned. "What is it?" Brianne asked.

"One of the major questions we had was how on earth Anita Turner could have found out about the Ebola vials being stored in the hospital."

"Yeah, so?"

"Well Rupert Jones was one of the eight people that knew about it. He could have told someone from the next room over and Anita could have overheard it."

Brianne's eyes widened. "Geez. You're telling me Mr. Charming over there's big mouth might be the entire reason there's an imminent threat of terrorism?"

I nodded. "I don't know for sure, of course. But that certainly would explain it."

"Just when I thought I couldn't like the guy any

less," Brianne muttered. "Do you think you're going to find the vials in time?"

I shrugged. "I honestly have no idea. Every minute that passes without us doing anything is agony, but I also know Violet and I can't do anything until tonight. Hopefully tomorrow morning the internet will be filled with people rejoicing that the vials have been found."

"I sure hope so," Brianne muttered. "Keep me up to date, will you?"

"Yeah, definitely."

"And in the meantime," she continued, "you should put an application in for medical school here. Your grades were good enough you'll be accepted, but it's too late to apply for the summer semester, you wouldn't start until January at the earliest. That gives you lots of time to decide if you really do want to go back to being a doctor, and you can always say no if you decide you want to become a detective or do something completely different."

"That's a good idea, thanks," I told Brianne, giving her a smile before finishing off the beer. "Hey, this is going to be a weird question, but do you own any good clothes for clubbing?"

wo hours later I was headed back to my place from Brianne's apartment, where she'd lent me some clothes that would hopefully be good for that night. We weren't exactly the same size, but it would be close enough, and seeing as the most risqué my current wardrobe got was a pair of Lululemon capris I used to go jogging three times when I decided on a whim I was going to get healthier–the downside to that was I'd forgotten that I thought running was invented as a special form of torture–and a tank top that I wore exclusively inside my apartment when it got to be too hot, which had had more food than I was willing to admit to spilled on it right now.

But, thanks to Brianne, I was now the proud owner of a tight, pastel pink skirt that ran about halfway down my thighs, a black halter top, more chunky jewellery than I ever expected to wear at once, and a pair of heels so high that just looking at them made me hope we were taking a cab to the club.

Violet texted me to come by any time before ten, as that was when we were leaving for the club, so I made my way to her place just after nine. I knew I was early, but I was anxious to find out where the Ebola vials were, before it was too late.

With Brianne's outfit and an hour spent making my hair nice and wavy, combined with my makeup done in shades I hadn't thought looked good since before I could legally drink, I definitely looked ready to hit the clubs. Looking at myself in the mirror, I didn't know if I'd say I looked *hot*–it certainly wasn't my favorite look in general–but I could definitely say I looked ready to hit the clubs like a twenty-two-year-old all over again.

"Don't worry Biscuit, I'm not bringing anyone home tonight," I reassured my cat before heading out. Seeing as he was curled up in a little ball in an old box on the floor, I didn't think he was that concerned.

What was immediately concerning was my skill in walking in Brianne's heels. In the sense that I had absolutely no skill at all at walking in them. I stumbled out the door like a drunk, giggling at my own complete inability to do something so simple as walking in heels. I hadn't worn any since the surgery on my knee, and even in the few years preceding that heels were maybe a once-a-year sort of thing. Medical school didn't exactly invite a thriving social life.

I looked at the four steps leading up to the street from my apartment dauntingly. Carefully, I made my way up them, feeling like a tightrope walker the whole time. But, I managed to make my way up all the steps without falling over onto the pavement. As I made my way toward Violet's house I started to slowly gain a tiny bit of confidence. After all, I'd made it a whole twenty yards without pitching forward into one of the neighbor's fences. That counted as a win, right? I made my way up to Violet's door and knocked. She yelled at me to come in, and I opened the door and practically collapsed onto the couch in her study.

"You are not used to the high heels, I presume?" Violet said with a small smile, making her way in from the kitchen.

"How do people stand on these all day?" I asked. "Not only do I feel like a circus freak, but my feet are killing me already!"

"If you really need them, I have flats that you may be able to get away with," Violet offered, but I shook my head.

"No, if we're clubbing, it has to be heels. I'm just being a big whiny baby about it. I'll be fine."

Violet was wearing a pair of high-rise black leggings with a black crop-top and an oversized flowery shirt on top of it. Her hair was tied up into a high pony, with strands of dark brown hair around her face. The scarlet lipstick contrasted well with her pale skin and dark hair.

"Good. We cannot go too early, however."

"Aren't you as nervous as I am?" I asked. "I mean, going to this club tonight, we might actually find out where the Ebola vials are being stored."

Violet shrugged. "What is the point in nerves? Either we will find the location of the vials, or we will not. There is no way to know until we get there, so no point in worrying about it. What I do know is that arriving at a club too early will appear suspicious, so our chances of a successful night improve by waiting for the correct time."

"I swear you're like 80 percent robot," I replied, Violet grinning in reply.

"I'll take it as a compliment, that comment."

"I didn't say it wasn't one," I replied as Violet made her way to her computer in the corner.

"This afternoon, I have done research on the club," Violet told me. "It is owned by a Serbian, Filip Petkovic. He is the head of a gang comprised mainly of Serbians or the children of immigrants from the region."

"So Dragan was a gang member?"

"Yes. They do not seem to be an especially violent gang; they generally attempt to smuggle drugs from the European mainland into the United Kingdom, but they are not the sort to be committing random acts of violence in the streets."

"I don't get it. Why would a Serbian gang want a whole bunch of Ebola vials?"

"They may want to return them back to their homeland. Tensions between the various ethnic groups in the former Yugoslav states have not disappeared. However, that would leave the people in the region they would be targeting—most likely Kosovo—quite vulnerable. We will see."

I really, really hoped these vials weren't going to be used to trigger another war in the Balkans, or whatever this gang hoped to achieve with it.

"Do you know how they found out Ed Harding had the vials?" I asked Violet, who shook her head no.

"I do not know that, no. But believe me; Lily's information is not wrong. If she led us to the Serbians, they are the ones who did it. As we gather more information, we will be better able to determine the details of how exactly the Ebola vials ended up in the hands of a Serbian gang."

Violet showed me a picture of Filip Petkovic; he was a man who looked to be around thirty, with black hair and deep-set eyes. "You need to know his face, in case we come across him in the club," Violet told me, and I nodded.

"Good. Now it is after ten. We can go now."

The two of us made our way slowly toward the main street, where we hailed a cab. Violet instructed it to take us directly to The Graffiti Club. I didn't even know that place had a name. The driver didn't know it, so Violet simply told him to make his way to Rupert Street and she would direct him from there.

Fifteen minutes later we were standing in the same spot we'd stood only a few hours before, and it couldn't have been more different.

Whereas the middle of the afternoon saw a small amount of traffic, comprising mainly of ambling tourists and businesspeople making their way to their destinations with purpose, this was very different.

Now, the office buildings around were all dark, the businesses closed for the day. The creatures of the night were out; young people looking to forget their troubles and dance the night away. A big guy who had to weigh at least three hundred pounds stood in front of the door Dragan had gone through, his legs spread apart and his arms crossed threateningly. People gathered in small groups around the front of the club, cackling with the laughter of the tipsy people who had been pre-drinking before making their way to the club.

Violet and I walked up to the bouncer. I actually managed to not embarrass myself completely walking in the shoes; Violet of course walked like a runway model in her four inch heels. I was starting to legitimately wonder if she actually *was* a robot and this was just some kind of weird experiment.

Surely nobody could be *that* good at practically everything.

Violet flashed the man a smile. "Sorry ladies, back of the line," the man said.

"But Filip said we could come straight in," Violet begged, changing her accent slightly. Was she pretending to be Serbian?

The man looked uncomfortably to the side, unsure as to whether or not his boss really wanted these two ladies in the club. Finally, deciding that two additional bodies was probably better than getting fired, he stepped aside.

"Have a good night," he said.

"*Hvala!*" Violet replied, and I smiled at him as we moved past and through the door.

I realized I was getting old when the first thing I thought when Violet and I made our way into the main part of the club was "Wow, the soundproofing in this building must have cost a fortune!"

The whole thing looked like a purple factory exploded. Everything was a different shade.

The bar at the far end of the room had neon purple lights shining upwards along the front of it. Violet spotlights shone around the room at random angles from the ceiling, where mauve cloth draped in soft waves toward the ground. A small VIP area at the back featured plum-colored chairs and tables. It was all incredibly overwhelming. The dance floor was filled with people dancing to the latest Shawn

Mendez remix while purple lights danced along with them.

"People come here willingly?" I practically shouted in Violet's ear in order to be heard.

"It does seem quite… excessive," she replied as we both looked around. Violet nodded toward a door at the far side of the room, right next to the bar. It read *EMPLOYEES ONLY* in big red letters. Apart from the entrance we'd just come in from, it seemed like the only other door anywhere in this club. Given as there were at least a hundred people on the dance floor, and more standing around and at the bar, I figured this place probably wasn't exactly up to the latest fire safety codes.

Violet and I meandered over to the door, but there were two people working behind the bar, only a few feet away, and it became instantly obvious that no matter how subtle Violet and I were, there was no way we were going to be able to make it through that door without at least one of them seeing us.

Looking over at the two people, I noticed the woman was making up a tray of drinks, probably to take to one of the VIP tables. I motioned for Violet to wait by the door for a minute while I made my way to the other side of the bar. It was so crowded in here that I had to squeeze past a few people, but that was fine. The more crowded things were, the better I expected my plan to work.

I hung around next to a group of young girls who

were giggling to themselves about how hot the bartender was when the waitress finally came by, carrying the tray of drinks precariously with one hand. I timed my 'accidental' bump into one of the girls perfectly; she was tipsy enough that she lost her balance and fell into the waitress, whose drinks all went flying.

I didn't stick around to see what happened next as everyone in the vicinity came over to have a look at what had happened. I pushed my way against the crowd and back to Violet, who gave me a nod of appreciation; looking back I saw that the second bartender had left his post to help clean up the broken glass that was now all over the floor.

Violet and I quickly opened the door to the employees' area and made our way inside, with no one having noticed.

"You are quick at thinking on your feet," Violet whispered as we made our way through the old, musty hallway. The soundproofing evidently extended to this part of the building as well; I could hear the light pounding of the beat from the other side of the door, but that was it. Seeing as it sounded like a fleet of jumbo jets taking off in there, that was impressive.

"Thanks," I said. "Although I have to say I took inspiration from when that actually happened to me once in undergrad. Except I was the one getting hit and taking out the poor waitress."

"I see you were not better with the high heeled shoes then either," Violet said, and I laughed quietly. We passed a closed door; Violet opened it to find it was simply an alcohol storage room. The next room was just a supply closet, but as soon as we opened the door to the third room, jackpot! It had filing cabinets, a desk, an old lamp on the table, and while it wasn't flashy by any stretch of the imagination, it obviously belonged to the manager.

Just as Violet and I were about to step inside, however, we heard someone call out.

"Hey, you two! What the hell are you doing here?"

This wasn't good.

CHAPTER 15

*V*iolet stopped and looked at the man. He was short, but heavyset. He had that kind of attitude that made you think that despite his shorter frame he'd be willing to go all out in a fight.

"I'm sorry," Violet said, going back to her usual French accent. "*Mon amie* and I, we look for bathroom?"

The man rolled his eyes. "Foreigners. Learn to speak English if you come to this country," he muttered under his breath, but still loudly enough for us to hear.

"No bathroom here," he said loudly. "You go back outside!" he ordered, pointing to the door.

"*Ah, les toilettes, ils sont la-bas?* The bathroom? Out there?" Violet asked once more. I had to admit she played the role of the clueless foreigner very well.

"No! No bathrooms! No bathrooms here. You

123

cannot be here. Go!" the man continued. He came closer to us, and when he was only a few feet away from where Violet and I were standing, she suddenly pulled a small black box from her purse and pointed it toward the man. A second later two wires spat out from the box toward him. When they connected with him his body went rigid, and a moment later he fell to the floor, the impact of his head hitting the ground knocking him unconscious.

"*Did you just tase him?*" I hissed at Violet, and she nodded.

"Yes."

"Oh my God. Why on earth do you have a *Taser* in your purse?"

"In case of situations like this, in which a man bigger than us wanted us to leave. Now, come. Help me put him in the storage room."

"These are *gangsters*. Jesus. They're probably going to kill us if they find out what we did."

"Relax," Violet replied. "This man is not a gangster. The children of immigrants do not complain about people who do not speak English; often their parents do not speak it. This is the type of man who drapes himself in the Union Jack and votes BNP. He is an employee, nothing more."

"You'd better be right," I muttered as Violet and I each grabbed one of the man's arms and dragged him toward the storage room. I fell onto my butt at one point; this was not the sort of thing I was expecting to have to do while wearing heels. After about three minutes, however, we had the man in the storage room, hidden behind a couple boxes of extra glasses. I double checked his pulse to make sure he wasn't going to die back there, then, satisfied that he was going to be fine, Violet and I made our way out of the room.

"Hopefully they do not find him for a while," Violet said as we made our way back to the office. "Given how hard his head hit the floor, I would not expect him to awaken in the next hour." Without wasting any time, we slipped inside the office and closed the door behind us, locking the deadbolt behind us just to be safe.

This time I got a better look around the room. The old desk in the center didn't have much on it, just a few pieces of unopened mail that looked like bills and a couple haphazardly placed pens. The cabinet against the far wall had a dead plant sitting on top of it. To my right was an armoire the size of a closet, presumably because gangsters need a change of clothes as well. On the left was a mini fridge, which Violet immediately opened. Unfortunately, there were only a few cans of beer in it.

"You'd think a guy who works fifty feet from the bar he owns wouldn't need to keep a cache of beer in his office, too," I noted, but even my joke had a tinge of sadness to it. As Violet had opened the fridge I'd felt my heart rate go up to dangerous new levels, but it was all for nothing. The Ebola vials weren't here, either.

"Sadly, I was not hoping to find beer in this fridge," Violet said, frowning as she sat back on her haunches for a moment before closing the door to the fridge and making her way to the desk. I opened the large armoire and found a few shirts hanging on hooks, along with a woman's jacket, when suddenly there was a sound at the door of someone trying to turn the knob.

I looked over at Violet, my eyes widening in panic. Shoot! What were we going to do?

"Damn it, I was sure I'd left the door unlocked," I heard a man's voice on the other side.

"Do you have your keys, boss?" someone else asked, as Violet immediately stood up and walked over to me. She shoved me into the armoire and walked in after me, pulling the door closed behind us. The light disappeared, along with all my hopes of ever getting out of here unnoticed, when I heard the jingling of a set of keys outside. A moment later the deadlock clicked and the door opened. Violet and I were no longer alone in this office.

My heart beat in my chest so hard I was sure the two men who had just entered the office would be able to hear it. Surely they were going to walk straight over here, open the doors, find Violet and I, and our bodies would eventually be discovered in a shallow grave somewhere, or washed up along the Thames.

I tried to force the images of my dead body out of my head and focus on what the two men were saying when they started talking.

"Bloody women, I tell you, Dragan. Never get married. They'll take over your life."

"Yes, boss," Dragan replied, and the first man laughed.

"You know, you can call me Filip. Everyone else does."

"If it's all the same to you."

"Now, I can't remember where the bloody hell I put the thing. This is ridiculous. The vials are being moved tonight, I should be there overseeing things. I had one foot out the door when Mira comes out and asks me to go out and get that stupid watch of hers that she left here the other day. I tell her I'm doing something important, she tells me doing what she wants is more important than anything I have to do. So now I've had to delay the shipment of the vials so I can get her stupid watch."

I couldn't help but smile at the conversation. I knew this guy was the head of a gang, and yet one word from his wife and he was actually changing his plans to move a deadly virus that his gang had killed someone over just because she wanted her watch back.

"Yeah, speaking of that, do you really think it's a

good idea to move the vials tonight? I mean, literally everywhere is talking about it. The BBC had someone from MI5 on earlier talking about how they're working with the London police to find the missing vials. MI5. That's some James Bond shit." I could practically feel Violet rolling her eyes next to me.

"Mate, look, I love you, but there's a reason you're the second in command," Filip said to Dragan. "You get up, you go get your slice of pizza from that frankly awful place by your flat, you come here, and you manage the club better than anyone else could. But the thing is, you don't have that natural risk-taking ability that you need to really get ahead in our business. That's why I do the big transactions. Yeah, it's risky. But you don't even have to do anything and when we pull this off you're getting a half a million quid. So relax, ok? It's going to be fine."

"Look, I get that. But the downside of this sort of thing is just huge. I saw on the TV they found Ed Harding's body today. You said they weren't going to. You said everything would be finished before they even knew he was dead."

"Yeah, so they got a copper who's slightly smarter than those other morons on it. There's literally nothing linking us to Harding. I searched his apartment before I left. Trust me. There's no chance we're getting caught here."

"Fine. So find your wife's stupid watch and we'll

get over to Aleks' place before they make the move without us. They can't wait forever, you know."

"Yeah, yeah. I'm on it. Listen, check and see if it's in the closet, will you? I think she might have left it in one of her jackets that's in there."

I felt the blood drain from my face instantly. As the footsteps came toward where Violet and I were hiding, I felt her hand touch my shoulder softly.

"You take Dragan," she whispered into my ear. "I'll take care of Filip."

Great. How on earth was I supposed to "take care" of Dragan? I had no idea, but I figured I'd better think of something fast, because the door to the armoire was about to open. At the last second, I thought I may as well use the element of surprise that I had at my disposal.

As soon as the armoire door began to open, I rammed into it with all the strength I could muster. There was a shout of surprise from Dragan and then a loud crack as the door hit him in the head. Instantly he crumbled to the ground as I heard the sound of Violet's Taser once more. I looked up to see Filip's eyes wide open as he was zapped, and I shook my head. When Violet finished Filip writhed on the floor. Violet took the lamp off his desk, ripped the cord from the socket and clocked him over the head with it. Filip stopped moving. It was only then that I realized in the pandemonium I'd broken the heel off one of my shoes. I'd never felt more like a superhero in my life; I'd broken a heel while taking out gangsters. I was basically Batman.

"You better not have killed him," I warned Violet as she made her way toward Filip.

"Relax," Violet replied. "It was a light blow. He is unconscious, no more. Same as Dragan."

I double checked to make sure she was right. "What do we do with them?" I asked. Violet pointed at Filip's size ten Adidas runners, and pulled a handful of cable ties out of her purse.

"I guess that is more useful than a lipstick top-up," I told her, grabbing a couple ties from her and making sure Dragan's arms and feet were secured. I turned him onto his side in case the hit from the armoire had concussed him, which might cause him to vomit when he woke up. Just because he was a gangster linked to a murderer didn't mean he deserved to die in a pool of his own vomit. I hadn't taken my Hippocratic Oath yet, but I still considered that 'first do no harm' applied to me as well.

"Come on," Violet told me. "Help me get them into the closet."

Together we dragged the two men–with much effort–into the closet and closed the door behind them. By the time we were done the thin sheen of sweat on my skin showed me just how much I needed to make exercise—beyond moving the unconscious bodies of criminals—a part of my daily routine.

"I have the cardio skills of a potato," I panted as Violet, looking as perfect as ever, smiled at me.

"Well, you should try to exercise more often than your current schedule of 'never,'" she replied, and I stuck my tongue out at her as I sucked up air.

"You're supposed to be supportive, not confirm it for me," I replied. "Now let's get out of here."

Violet nodded and we left the room, making sure no one was following us. Carrying my broken shoes, we made our way back to the street, and walked to Shaftesbury Avenue to meld in with the crowds a little bit better.

Violet took out her phone. "We have to call DCI Williams."

I wondered how on earth Violet was going to explain what we'd done without admitting to any crimes.

CHAPTER 16

"*T*his had better be important, it's almost midnight," DCI Williams said as soon as he picked up. Violet had put the call on speakerphone so I could listen in as well.

"If it was not important, I would not call you." I heard DCI Williams sigh on the other end of the line.

"What is it, Violet?"

"Well, for one thing, the man who killed Edward Harding is currently, shall we say, indisposed, in the club that he owns on Rupert Street."

"What? Are you serious? Of course you're serious, you've never made a joke in your life. Jesus, how on earth did you figure that one out?"

"It does not matter right now. You will have all the answers for your police report eventually. That is not all. I need you to send a hazardous materials team to the home of a member of the gang *Serbian Dragon* named Aleksander to find the Ebola virus."

"What's his last name?"

"I do not know yet. We only discovered this information minutes ago."

"And how, exactly, did you get the information?"

"We overheard a conversation between the leader of the Serbian Dragons, Filip Petkovic, and his second-in-command Dragan. They said that the Ebola vials are at the home of a man named Aleksander, who presumably is a part of their gang, and that they will be moving the vials shortly. I do not have time to explain everything, but you need to get a warrant for the place right now."

"Christ, Violet, it's the middle of the night."

"If you tell the judge that should a terrorist attack occur because he wanted to sign warrants during business hours only he will be responsible for whatever happens, I am certain that he will be significantly less upset with you, and significantly more inclined to sign your piece of paper."

"I'll try," DCI Williams said. "But I can't promise you anything. You know that."

"I am aware," Violet said, hanging up the phone. "We need to find a computer," she said suddenly. "There is an internet café only one hundred meters from here, the Candy Café, but it closed at eleven thirty."

"So what are we going to do?" I asked. Violet suddenly began practically running down the street until we reached a certain apartment block. When we reached the front door she buzzed one of the numbers, holding her finger down on the button for a good thirty seconds before finally a sleepy-sounding female voice came through the loudspeaker.

"If this is a prank, I'm calling the police."

"It is not a prank," Violet replied.

"Damn it," the voice on the other end said. "What do you want, Violet?"

"Let me up, I need your computer."

Without any more conversation, a moment later the door buzzed, letting us in. We went up the old, rickety stairs to the second floor and to apartment eight. Violet knocked and a moment later the door opened. Standing in front of us was a rather annoyed-looking woman in her forties.

"It's the middle of the night, Violet," the lady said to us. She was wearing only a thick terry-cloth bathrobe.

"I only came here because it's an emergency. I need to use your computer. Go back to bed, we'll let ourselves out."

"Good," the lady replied, closing the door behind us as we entered her apartment. It was fairly bare-bones, a one bedroom with a small couch and coffee table in the living room, a TV on a stand and a computer at the desk in the corner. A couple of cheap art prints lined the walls, but it was obvious that the woman didn't put much effort into keeping the place neat and tidy. Violet immediately made her way over there while the lady went into the bedroom and closed the door.

"Who is she?" I asked Violet quietly as she booted up the computer.

"Valerie was a client once. She wanted my help, and I gave it to her. Unfortunately for her, she wasn't happy with the result. In the end, the person attempting to take her life was her ex-husband, and she has not forgiven me for sending him to prison. However, she is aware that she owes me a debt, which is why we are now using her computer."

"Wow," I replied. "That's crazy."

"It is not crazy, statistically a woman is most likely to be murdered by the man with whom she lives."

"Well yeah, I know that, but still. I've never met someone whose husband tried to kill her."

"Most likely because most of them are successful. Her husband was a coward and a moron. He did not want to be arrested for her murder so chose to do so through poisoning her food–he was a chef. He was so bad at it that it did not kill her, it only made her sick. It gave me the time I needed to prove that her husband was the murderer-to-be, and have him arrested."

At this point the computer started up, and Violet's

fingers flew across the keyboard. She opened up a window in Google Chrome and straight away opened about ten tabs; I noticed Facebook and Instagram to name a couple. She began to scroll through things at a rate faster than I could make out before finally, about twenty minutes later, she let out a triumphant "aha!"

"Did you find out where Aleks lives?" I asked, and Violet nodded.

"Yes." She pulled out her phone and called DCI Williams once more. "I know where Aleksander lives," she told him.

"Yes, well, it doesn't matter," DCI Williams replied. "The judge we woke up won't give us a warrant to search a man's home based on your word alone."

"Did you tell him that it may result in the prevention of a terrorist attack on British soil?"

"I did, but the reply was that we cannot simply ignore our laws to suit us."

"Fine. Go to Petkovic's club. He is in his manager's office, locked in a closet."

"We found him there already. Along with Dragan and a security worker named Kevin Chapman in a supply closet. Petkovic wants to press charges against you. He says you tased him."

"Criminals, they lie! That is what they do. Where would I have got a Taser from, anyway?"

"And yet for some reason I'm inclined to believe

him. Maybe it's the taser marks on his chest. Regardless, he's asked for an attorney and refuses to speak with us. He deleted all his text messages; we can't find anything on his phone that might prove the Ebola vials are at Aleksander's house."

"If all you have is bad news, then get off the phone and stop wasting my time," Violet said.

"All right, I'll call you in the morning if we have something."

The call disconnected, and Violet stood up. We left the apartment, closing the door behind us, and made our way back to the streets, where Violet immediately hailed a cab.

"Cresset Road, Hackney," she told the cabbie. "There's an extra fifty quid in it for you if you get us there in under twenty minutes."

The cabbie took off from the curb so fast I felt myself thrown back against the seat. We were definitely going to make Violet's twenty minute timeline, if we didn't die in a fiery wreck first.

"Aleksander's home?" I asked, and Violet nodded, her eyes gleaming with excitement.

"We have a window, here. It is a small window; they are moving the vials soon. If the police will do nothing about it, we will have to."

"And how, exactly, are we going to break into an apartment filled with gangsters getting ready to move vials of a deadly virus somewhere else?" I asked, quietly enough so that the cabbie wouldn't hear.

Violet shrugged. "I do not know, but we have just under twenty minutes to come up with a plan."

This definitely didn't sound like the sort of thing that was going to end well.

CHAPTER 17

*H*ackney was well known as being one of London's more crime-ridden neighborhoods, and as soon as we got there I could tell it was completely different from the rest of London. Whereas the inner city was made up of classy, gorgeous buildings, the sort of thing you see on postcards, Hackney seemed to mainly comprise of large brick apartment buildings, the sort of thing that were all over the place in the sixties and seventies. If they'd been concrete instead of brick they could have been mistaken for Soviet communist apartments.

The local council had obviously made an effort to clean the place up a little bit by planting large trees with plush leaves, but even their branches looked slightly droopy and depressed in the night.

Litter was scattered along the roads and groups of young men loitered in the shadows. The sound of

SAMANTHA SILVER

firecrackers on a street nearby made me jump. This wasn't the kind of place that I'd want to spend a lot of time around at night, that was for sure.

I tried not to think about that as Violet and I made our way toward the building. The name, Milborne House, made it sound like a classy kind of place. It was the absolute opposite of that. Made of dirty red bricks, about five stories tall, with a front door painted bright blue, the building actually reminded me a bit of my old elementary school, in one of the worst parts of San Francisco. Two men were loitering out the front of the building, smoking pot.

The two men leered at us as we made our way to the front door. Violet smiled seductively at one of them.

"I'm trying to surprise my boyfriend," she told them, putting the French accent on even more heavily than usual. "Would you mind buzzing us into the building?"

"Yeah, no worries," one of the men replied, not hiding the fact that he was looking directly down her top. He was so busy staring at Violet's cleavage that he practically walked into the door himself, and as they let us into the building I could sense the stares of both men on our rear ends.

"If you ladies decide you want some more fun, we'll be here," one of them called out after us, and I shuddered.

140

"Why didn't you just crack the code yourself?" I asked Violet.

"Did you see the amount of dirt on that keypad? It would have taken me ages; dealing with Mister Charming down there was far more efficient. Aleksander lives in apartment 1F, likely on the first floor."

We made our way up the stairs–I still didn't have any shoes and made a mental note to get a tetanus booster tomorrow just in case–and a few minutes later found ourselves in front of the apartment we wanted. Violet pulled out her tools and quietly unlocked the door. If I'd learned anything from being around her, it was that it was *way* easier to break into places than I'd ever realized. When I bought my own home one day there were going to be like, at least six deadbolts on the door.

I had no idea what we were going to find when we entered the apartment. I supposed I shouldn't have been surprised when it wasn't empty; as soon as we entered the small, one-bedroom apartment it was obvious he'd spotted us, too.

Black hair, tanned face, tattoos all over his arms and chest–what I could see of them, anyway–and eyes that immediately darted toward the window. This guy's fight-or-flight reaction tended toward flight. At least that boded well for us.

A second later, however, after realizing that rather than being burly gangsters we were two young women, one of whom wasn't wearing shoes, with neither one of us wearing clothing that was especially handy to be fighting in, he decided that maybe fighting was his best option. He began to run, obviously intending to blow through us and out the door rather than jump out the window.

I froze. After all, this man who weighed probably almost twice what I did was rushing toward me. I had no idea what he was going to do. Was he going to hit us? Knock us out? Did he have a knife hidden that he was going to pull out? No, my fight-or-flight response was apparently completely broken.

Violet's, on the other hand, was fine. She carefully took a step to the side as the man ran past her, then held out her ankle as he went soaring through the air, completely out of control, crumpling against the wall on the other side of the hallway.

The man groaned as Violet stepped out into the hall, grabbed him by the shirt collar, and dragged him back into the apartment, closing the door behind her, then dropped him back onto the ground, where his head hit the carpet and he writhed around.

"Who the hell are you two?" the man asked groggily. I was fairly certain he had a mild concussion.

"Oh no, I think you do not understand. We are the ones asking the questions. Is the Ebola gone?"

"What Ebola?"

"You do not need to play dumb with me, it is evident you are an idiot already. The Ebola that the others left with, where did they go?"

"I don't know what you're talking about," the man replied groggily. Violet sighed and reached into her purse, pulling out the Taser.

"And now? Are you still going to pretend to be dumber than you really are?"

"Jesus," the man said, scrambling along the ground to back further away from Violet. "Look, I don't know where they went, I swear."

"Is that your final answer?" Violet asked, leveling the Taser at the man's chest.

"Yes! Yes, I swear I don't know where they went. I admit, I had the vials here. They were here until about twenty minutes ago. We were supposed to wait for Filip, but he should have been here an hour ago, so we had to move them without him. But I swear, they did not tell me where they were going. They took the virus in a car. Maybe to give to the buyer?"

"What do you know about the buyer?" Violet asked.

"I… I don't know anything!" the man said, pressing himself against the wall, as though if he wished hard enough he might simply disappear into it. Violet narrowed her eyes and moved her finger to the Taser's trigger, and the man began to panic.

"Wait! Wait! I know… I know he's from London. I know he's planning something big. Our guys are doing everything for him, in exchange for the big payday. We're getting ten million, total, for our role in this. That's all I know, I swear!"

"Give me your mobile," Violet ordered, and the man reached into his back pocket with a trembling hand, passing his phone to Violet.

"Do you need the passcode?" the man asked, and Violet smirked.

"Please," she replied with a scoff, and I couldn't help but smile. A second later I saw the screen flash to life as Violet had unlocked the phone, and she began to go through it. As she did so, I looked around the apartment. It was fairly Spartan, with a stained couch on one side of the living room, a huge plasma TV on the other side, and mess everywhere. On the ottoman was a pizza box I was pretty sure was at least a few days old, a Chinese take-out menu that had been ripped in half lay abandoned on the carpet and what I was fairly certain was a dirty pair of boxers hung off a plastic chair in the corner of the room. Ew.

Violet scanned through the phone, then, evidently unhappy with what she found, threw it back at the man on the ground as I made my way to the kitchen. I had to check the fridge, just in case, even though the man had already said the others had left with the Ebola vials. Sure enough, the fridge was basically empty.

I sighed and shook my head at Violet.

"And you know nothing else of the man paying you for the vials, nor where the men with the vials have gone?"

The man shook his head and Violet sighed again. She picked up his phone, which was still sitting on the man's chest. "I am taking this. Do not contact your friends. Also, you should make an effort to visit your mother more often. Just because she lives in Yorkshire does not mean you should ignore her; she obviously cares about you."

Leaving the man gaping, awestruck, at Violet, we turned and left. I was too worried about the Ebola to even bother asking Violet how she knew that stuff about the man's mother. Making our way through the streets, I barely noticed the loiterers and catcallers; I was just bummed out that once again we'd missed our chance at finding the vials. Violet checked the man's phone every five seconds or so; I was sure she was waiting for someone to text so she could reply and hopefully get some more information.

When we finally got into the cab I leaned back against the seat. It was now almost two in the morning.

"Please tell me you noticed something. Anything," I begged Violet, who shook her head sadly.

"Nothing important. I am afraid that I must admit I am completely at a loss. I do not know where they took the vials."

She called DCI Williams and put the phone on speaker.

"What do you have for me?" he asked immediately.

"Aleksander is still at his home, although the vials are gone. They left twenty minutes ago. I do not know where."

DCI Williams let out a loud sigh. "Well, Petkovic and Blagojevic have both asked for lawyers. They're refusing to speak to us."

"I am sorry to say that they may be the only two people left to whom we have access to who know what has happened to the Ebola. My suspicion is that if there will be an attack, it will be in the next twenty-four hours."

"Yes, well, unlike you, I don't have the liberty of ignoring the law whenever it suits me. I'll do what I can, Violet. But don't hold your breath."

"They are being paid ten million pounds for the theft of the vials," Violet said. "They have a buyer. This is not a case of extreme nationalism; they are in this for the money. Use that information as you will."

"Thanks," DCI Williams said. "Keep me posted if you find out anything else."

The call ended, along with most of my hopes that we were going to find the vials in time.

"Now what do we do?" I asked.

"Well, you must go to bed. After all, you must go to the presentation Jake is doing tomorrow morning."

"Ok, one, how did you know I was going to that? I

haven't told you anything about it. And two, how am I supposed to go watch a presentation while knowing that at any moment Ebola might be launched into this town?"

"You will go because there is nothing to be done. There is no point in worrying about anything, because you cannot do anything about it. Going about your normal life is the best thing you can do. As to how I know, I saw the email that Jake sent you."

I narrowed my eyes. "When did you see it?"

"I was doing some mindless computer exercises the other night, as I was thinking about this case. I would have seen it then."

"So in normal people terms, you hacked my email?"

"Yes. But do not worry, I only read the one from Jake."

"Oh, well as long as you only invaded my privacy a *little bit*," I replied, rolling my eyes.

"I needed something easy to hack, as a palette cleanser," Violet explained. Of course it was just like her to justify it rather than apologize.

"So you're saying my email was easy to hack. You're not making things better for yourself, here."

Violet shrugged. "You are the one who uses your cat's name and birth year as a password. I cannot be blamed if anyone with a passing knowledge of your life can figure it out."

Making a mental note to change my password, I

leaned my head back against the headrest. The adrenaline from the night was wearing off, and my body was overcome by a sudden wave of pure exhaustion.

"You know, I'm too tired to deal with this right now," I said. "Stop reading my emails."

"That is fine, all you had to do was ask," Violet said.

"And don't hack any of my private accounts in the future, either," I added, glaring at her.

"All right, all right," she said, putting her arms up. Sometimes, dealing with Violet was absolutely impossible.

$\mathcal{I}$ remembered to set my alarm in time to get to Jake's presentation the next morning, which thankfully wasn't until eleven. Even so, I was so tired when the alarm finally went off that I mashed the snooze button enough times so that when I finally got up, I was running late.

Throwing my hair up into a ponytail rather than shower, I quickly took off all the makeup from the night before that I'd been too tired to remove before going into bed, replaced it with much more daytime-appropriate shades and amounts, fed Biscuit and ran out the door.

Glancing at my phone when I reached Euston station, I saw I had just enough time to grab a quick latte from a cart vendor on the street before making my way to where Jake was holding his lecture: the UCL Cruciform Building.

Now, as a proud Stanford student, I was always ready to tell anyone, anywhere, anytime about the beauty of the campus and how no other University campus on earth came close to the incredible beauty of where I went. But I had to admit, as I came across the Cruciform building, my breath caught in my throat.

It was incredible. Five stories high, the gothic-style building towered over the street. Built with bricks in so deep a shade of red they were almost brown, the roof was topped with copper that had long since oxidized green. White brick made decorative accents, and the white frames of the windows added even more class to the building. Brass letters across the top entrance announced 'University College London' and above that was a seal with the letters MDCCCV. It took me a minute to remember my roman numeral conversions, and realize this building dated from 1805.

I realized I was staring and was going to be late, and quickly made my way inside.

The interior of the building was like a cross between a modern building and a historic one. In some ways, it felt like I'd just been transported to Hogwarts. Roman arches, mosaic floors, brick walls and iron balustrades, combined with warm lighting gave the interior a magical feel, while at the same time the wooden doors, occasional tiled floors and plastered walls did remind me that this was the twenty-first century after all. It was a beautiful mixture of modern and ancient, and I found myself looking around in awe as I made my way toward the classroom where Jake was giving his speech.

When I walked into the room, I had to admit I was surprised. It was completely modern; six rows of long tables with benches ran in a semi-circle around the room; the center had a large projection screen, with purple carpet flooring. Small lights in the ceiling beamed down on the room, which was filled with maybe one hundred and fifty students, their voices as they chatted to one another filling the room with a low, buzzing sound. I knew this scene all too well.

Finding a seat near the back of the room, I pulled out my phone to see if I'd received any last minute texts from Violet, telling me she had solved everything and saved the country from a potential terrorist attack. Unfortunately, my screen's background–a picture I'd taken of Biscuit trying to steal a slice of pizza from the counter–announced no new text messages. I sighed as I turned my phone to silent just as Jake walked into the room.

True to form, the buzzing didn't exactly stop, but it dropped in volume significantly as Jake made his way to the front of the room. I smiled to myself as I noticed the groups that had stopped talking and were now giving this new speaker their undivided attention were almost exclusively female–and one group of obviously gay men.

"All right everyone, if I can get your attention," Jake said, his voice carrying across the room without need for a microphone. He waited for a minute and the noise slowly dimmed to silence.

"Thank you. First of all, I'd like to introduce myself. My name is Jake Edmunds, and I'm a pathologist at the Westminster Public Mortuary."

An excited buzz passed through the room at those words. Obviously this was the first time these students had encountered someone who worked with the dead, rather than the living.

"That's right," Jake said. "When you guys screw up, they send them to me, and I'm the one who's going to nail you to the wall for it."

"I'd let you nail me against the wall any day," one girl called out, as the whole class burst out into laughter. I saw a blush creeping up Jake's face as he looked around the room and his eyes locked on mine. I laughed and waved. Evidently relieved, Jake cleared his throat.

"Why do you think they got me to lecture you on pathology?" Jake said, ignoring the remark as the laughter died down. "There's usually not that much to laugh about in my line of work. I do get to work with the police, though. And there are some characters who show up in my office that way. Some of them are pretty cute, too," he continued, looking at me again, and this time it was my turn to blush.

For the next hour and fifteen minutes Jake continued his speech about pathology, and I actually gained quite a bit of insight into exactly what it was he did. While I'd seen autopsies performed in medical school it was all very clinical and sanitized; Jake managed to humanize it quite a bit. He mentioned how he always took care with people, knowing that when they were murdered their bodies were left with very little dignity, and that he did his best to treat bodies with respect, knowing that there was always someone out there who cared. And even if there wasn't, Jake explained, he cared. He was taught to treat people with dignity, and he thought that applied to both the living and the dead.

By the time the lecture ended, I realized every single eye in the room was pasted onto Jake. Unsurprisingly, he had been an incredibly charismatic speaker. As the students filed out of the room–I noticed at least three girls and one man asking him mundane questions at the end just to slip him their phone numbers–I hovered at the back of the room and waited for it to empty. Finally, as the last person left, I made my way toward Jake.

"So?" he asked, grinning. "What did you think?"

"I think you just helped create a whole bunch of competition for yourself," I answered. "Half this class is going to want to do what you do now."

Jake laughed. "That's good, right?"

"That's very good. You were awesome. I mean it."

"Well, now that you've said that, I can get rid of these," Jake replied with a wink, tossing the pieces of paper he'd been given by students with their phone numbers into the trash.

"Just hedging your bets in case I said you were awful?" I teased, and Jake laughed.

"Yup, for sure. I thought the guy was kind of cute."

I snuggled my arm into his as we headed back out toward the exit. "Do you want to grab a quick lunch or something?" Jake asked, and I nodded.

"Sure, but I might beg off at any minute. I haven't heard from Violet yet, but if she texts, I'll have to go."

"Of course. So you haven't found the vials yet?" he asked quietly, and I shook my head.

"No. We almost got them last night, we ended up at a club owned by Serbian gangsters, and then the apartment of one of his compatriots, but they had already moved the vials." We ended up walking to a Pizza Express nearby and got seated by the window where we could watch the passersby as we spoke.

"I need to know the rest of that story," Jake told me. "Serbian gangsters? Really?"

"I wish I was joking. They're the ones who have the vials now."

"Any idea what they're going to do with them?" Jake asked, concerned, and I shook my head.

"No. We're out of ideas. Violet said she's going to spend the rest of the time we have thinking."

"Well, her brain is her biggest asset. But when you say you guys snuck into a gangster's club, you're being safe about it, right? I mean, I'm happy for you to go off and solve crimes with Violet, but this sounds dangerous."

"It's ok," I replied. "Violet brought a Taser, which she put to good use."

Jake burst out laughing. "Of course she did. I wonder where she got a Taser from."

"Probably stole it from one of the cops. Did you know she has a whole collection of stolen police badges?"

"I did not know that, no. That's insane. Tell me the whole story though, I need to know this."

By the time I'd gotten through the whole thing Jake was practically in tears, and it wasn't from the jalapenos on the pizza.

"I know I'm not supposed to find this funny, since there's now a very real threat of an attack, but I just can't help it. Everything about your adventure last night is amazing."

"I'll probably be able to find it funny if we manage to find the Ebola *before* anything bad happens."

"Yeah, I get that. And you really have no idea where it could be?"

"None whatsoever. I'm not even bothering to try

and figure this out. If Violet can't do it, then there's no way I'll be able to."

"What about if you see her creepy sister again?" Jake asked. "I remember when her husband was killed. I never made the connection that she was actually related to Violet."

"I don't think the sister will actually know this. She knew the Serbians were involved, but this is getting into the details."

"Yeah, you're right. Well, hopefully the lawyers will convince Petkovic and Dragan to give up the location."

"I hope so," I said, but I wasn't really holding out that much hope.

"So," Jake continued. "Are you going to go back to med school and become a pathologist now that you've heard my riveting description of the job?"

I laughed. "Honestly, I'm not really interested in working with the already dead. Although, I have been considering maybe putting an application in to go back to medical school."

"Oh yeah?" Jake asked, and I recounted my conversation with Brianne.

"I think that's a great idea," Jake told me. "This way you don't have to make a decision straight away, but the option is there for you if you decide to take it."

"Yeah," I said. "I'm just not sure yet. I mean, I can't sit around doing nothing for the rest of my life. And sure, playing Sherlock Holmes with Violet is a lot of fun, but I don't help her with all of her cases, and I feel like I have a lot to offer the world other than playing tourist here in London."

"I know what you mean," Jake said. "And it's good that you're starting to feel this way. It means you're starting to get through your depression more fully. I've already noticed that you seem a lot more energetic than when I first met you. This is good."

"I know," I said quietly, nodding. "I'm happy about that."

Jake reached over and took my hand. "If you ever need anything, anything at all. I'm here, remember?"

"Thanks," I told him with a smile. "I know. And I appreciate it."

Right then and there, I felt like the luckiest woman alive.

CHAPTER 19

*E*ventually Jake had to get back to the morgue, and I had to get back to my worried panicking about the potential terrorist attack. I made my way back to Eldon Road, but rather than go into my own apartment, I knocked on the door of Violet's house.

"Come in!" Violet called from inside, and I opened the door and walked in. I was sure Violet had to have security cameras watching her front door; there was no way she could know it was me, otherwise, and quite frankly in Violet's line of work leaving the front door unlocked with no extra security had to be a bad idea. But, no matter how hard I looked, I could never see the cameras that I knew had to be there.

When I got to Violet's study, I stopped. Violet was sitting in the middle of the floor, legs crossed, eyes closed, like some kind of yoga guru. Around her was what looked like about half a forest worth of paper. Every inch of the floor was covered, and what didn't fit on the floor had been tacked onto the wall and bookcases, so that nearly every inch of the room was now completely white.

"Did a tree explode in your study or something?" I asked, moving into the kitchen and grabbing a chair, and bringing it back to the study. I placed the chair on the edge of the pile of papers and sat down. Violet opened her eyes and stretched her arms upwards.

"No, I asked DCI Williams to send me a copy of everything he had on this case. Apparently the police thought the paperwork was more important than actual investigation. I added my own discoveries as well. Now I have everything we know about this case here."

"And you're trying to figure it out through osmosis?" I asked, picking up the sheet closest to me. It was a police report on an old arrest of Filip Petkovic for a suspected robbery. The charges were eventually dropped due to a lack of evidence.

"I am trying to figure it out by thinking. There must be something that we have missed. Something to help us find the rest of the men. Something to help us figure out exactly who is behind all of this. Something to help us discover where they have taken the vials."

"That sounds like as good a reason as any to keep thinking," I said with a small smile, grabbing another sheet of paper off the floor. This one was a list of all the people suspected to be a part of Petkovic's gang. There were about thirty names on it, and they were listed in order of hierarchy, with Petkovic on top, Dragan just below him and Aleksander a few names under that. Suddenly, I had an idea!

"What about tracking their phones?" I suddenly asked excitedly. "We have their names. Do your hacking magic and find out what cell phone companies they're with, and then track them with the GPS," I said to Violet, who shook her head sadly.

"I do like the idea, especially since I thought of it around six hours ago. I have the numbers for all the men of the phones registered in their names, but they have all been turned off; none of them are leaving a signal."

My shoulders slumped. I had been so excited for a minute that maybe we could solve this whole case that way. Still, there was absolutely no way I was going to give up now.

"Come," Violet said as she got up and made her way to the kitchen at the back of the house. "I have not eaten anything since last night, my brain requires sustenance in order to function at its peak, and I would be willing to bet that you have not eaten anything remotely healthy in longer than that. The change in setting may prove to stimulate the brain as well."

"Hey," I said, frowning. "I do too eat healthy."

"What was the last thing you ate?"

"I had pizza with Jake for lunch after his presentation. Pizza that had meat *and* vegetables on it."

Violet rolled her eyes. "And before that?"

"Ummm," I said, thinking back. "The pizza we ate at that hole in the wall."

"Yes, it is evident from your answers that your eating habits are the pinnacle of health."

"The food pyramid is shaped like a pizza, so it counts as healthy."

"The smoothie I am going to make you does not only *count* as healthy, it actually *will be* healthy," Violet said, grabbing spinach out of the fridge.

"I don't want vegetables in my smoothie," I whined, realizing a little bit too late *just* how much like a two year old I really sounded. Violet raised an eyebrow. "Please," I added lamely.

"Fine," she said. "I will make you a mixed berry smoothie." She reached into the fridge and pulled out punnets of blackberries, strawberries, raspberries and blueberries.

"Are you seriously going to eat all of that before it goes bad?" I asked. I knew fruit was in season, with it being summer and all, but that still seemed excessive.

"Yes, because I am an adult, and unlike you I eat like one," Violet told me, piling an individual blender cup full of berries, then adding flax seeds, a thick yogurt called Skyr—"it comes from Iceland, it is like regular yogurt, only thicker"—and almond milk, and blending it all together. Violet poured the smoothie in a glass and handed it to me, and I took a sip. It was delicious, but I wasn't about to go and admit that straight away.

"That's all right," I said, and Violet nodded.

"Good. Eat all of it. You will feel better afterwards." I watched as she piled her smoothie full of spinach, kiwi fruit and mango, added the Skyr, flax seeds and almond milk, then blended it into a smooth mixture.

"You see? You have eaten vitamins, and you are not dead," Violet said, motioning to my half-empty smoothie a minute later, and I stuck my tongue out at her. We moved to the breakfast bar and I sat on one of the antique-style stools next to Violet. Her whole home had a rustic feel to it; the kind of place that made you feel like there were hidden secrets.

And knowing Violet, there were definitely hidden secrets in this home. There just had to be.

"What I do not like about this case is the number of questions we still have unanswered," Violet said, staring into her smoothie like it was a crystal ball with all the answers.

"Like how the Serbians found out Artie Ingram, or Ed Harding, or whatever we want to call him, had the Ebola vials in the first place," I replied.

"*Exactement*," Violet replied, nodding. "We have moved forward in the case, but we have left so many blanks along the way. Who did the Serbians steal the vials for? Why did their purchaser not steal them themselves?"

"Aren't there hidden terrorists, members of ISIS, living in the UK?" I asked Violet.

"Yes, but they are generally not the types of people who can afford to spend ten million pounds on something. And I cannot picture them using Christians as allies. Something here does not make sense."

"It's almost like someone is paying them to commit a terrorist attack so they can make money off it, but that's stupid. No one makes money off a terrorist attack."

Violet suddenly looked at me, her eyes flashing.

"Oh, but that is where you are wrong. Cassie, you are a *génie!*" She jumped up off the stool and began pacing the room. "We have been looking at this all wrong. This whole time, we have been assuming that someone wants to commit the attacks for ideological reasons, but *what if that is not the case?* What if it is, as you say, for money?"

"But how would someone make money off a terrorist attack?"

"Think, Cassie. What happens when there is an attack on a country? What do people do?"

I began to think back to the terrorist attacks I knew the most about–9/11 obviously. There were the attacks in Paris a while back. There were the bombings here in London about ten years ago.

"People get scared, they stop traveling," I said slowly.

"*Oui*," Violet said. "So what does that do to companies?"

"Well, travel company stocks would drop. Maybe oil as well, if people aren't traveling as much."

"And insurance," Violet added. "The drops are not necessarily long-lasting, but they are there."

"So if someone knew a terrorist attack was going to happen, they could play the market?"

"Exactly. The easiest way to do it is to 'short' a stock–essentially betting that a certain company's stock price will drop. If it does, you make money. If it rises, you lose money."

"Does this mean that job interview Ingram went to…" I said, my voice trailing off as I remembered the options trader we interviewed a few days ago.

"Yes," Violet nodded. "How was I such an idiot? It was so obvious, it was right in front of me. Come. We go to the City."

My heart pounded in my chest as we practically sprinted out the door, the smoothies forgotten. We were going to find out what the Serbians planned to do with the Ebola vials.

CHAPTER 20

iolet texted DCI Williams as we sped down toward the offices where Anthony Roman worked.

"I have been such an *imbécile*," Violet muttered to herself. "The answer was right there. I should have seen it earlier."

"Well, as long as we still get to the vials in time, no harm no foul," I said to Violet, trying to make her feel better, but she just shook her head.

"No. No, it is not only about the vials. It is about my methods. I made a mistake. I do not make mistakes."

"Everyone makes mistakes."

"I am not everyone," Violet sniffed. "But no matter. For now, we go and we do what we can to get the information we can on where the vials are now."

The cabbie pulled up in front of the office building. Violet threw him a fifty-pound note and we sprinted out of the cab and into the building. This time, Violet didn't bother with the receptionist, the two of us walking briskly past her as she protested behind us.

"Hey! You can't go in there!"

Ignoring her, Violet and I strode down the hallway and straight into Anthony Roman' office. He was on the phone, and this time, when he looked up and saw us, he was visibly annoyed. Ignoring us, he typed on his computer at a rapid pace, while still talking to whoever was on the other end of the line.

"Come back after the market is closed," he begged, still typing away frantically. Violet walked calmly over to the wall where a large powerboard–one of the ones with a thousand different switches and surge protectors–was plugged into the wall. She grabbed the cord in the power outlet and pulled it out. Immediately the hum from the computers and monitors in the room all dulled.

"What the hell?" Anthony Roman cried out, his phone call forgotten. "What do you think you're doing?"

"We need to talk to you, and your attention was sadly focused elsewhere. Please, sit."

"I'm not going to sit. You can't come into my office and do this," Roman said, moving to the wall and plugging his cords back in. "I'll have your badge."

Violet smiled. "It will be difficult to do from prison."

"What the hell are you talking about? You can't come in here and threaten me with jail time."

"I can when you are willing to pay a Serbian gang ten million pounds to release Ebola virus on London so that you can capitalize on the immediate market drop in the aftermath."

Roman stopped suddenly at Violet's words. Evidently they had the intended effect.

"What?" he finally managed to stammer out, moving back to his chair and practically collapsing in it.

"The game is up," Violet told him. "I know everything."

"There's nothing to know. I'm not involved in any of this."

"The police are waiting downstairs to arrest you. I am here simply as a courtesy. I know that you are the one behind all of this."

"No. No, you're wrong. I don't know where you got this idea."

"All right, you do not believe me. Since I need to know where the vials are, let me explain everything that happened to you. When you realize just how much I know, you will answer the rest of my questions, and maybe– just maybe–you will not spend the entirety of the rest of your life in prison."

Violet leaned back in the chair comfortably, like a parent about to tell a child a fairy tale.

"It all started when Anita Turner told her boyfriend, the man whom she knew as Edward Harding, about what she had overheard in the hospital: for three days, the hospital was to store Ebola vials. Now, Anita thought her boyfriend was a regular man, but he was not. He was a thief; a thief who had stolen from the wrong man in Russia, and was now lying low in England for a few years before moving back to his old life in Eastern Europe. The man knew what the vials would be worth, and quite frankly, he could not resist."

Violet's eyes turned hard. "But the main problem he would have was getting rid of them. How could he get in touch with someone who wanted the vials? Harding turned to his connections overseas, looking for someone who would pay good money for vials of a disease that could spread terror. And his connection sent him to you, a fellow Russian."

Anthony Roman scoffed. "I'm more English than either one of you. I was born in Manchester. I went to Eton, and then Cambridge. I've lived in London almost my whole life."

"And yet your handkerchief, obviously a present from your mother, given the fact that you still carry it with you despite its age and the overly feminine pattern, is monogrammed AP."

"Yes, my mother gave me the handkerchief as a

gift years ago. She passed away eight years ago now, and the rest of the letter 'R' has been worn off."

"That is what I thought at first, but no, it has become evident that you are lying. Your name is Anthony Roman–or Anton Romanov, to be more exact–and in the Cyrillic alphabet, the Roman letter 'R' is written as a 'P'. Your parents are Russian."

Anthony Roman just stared at Violet for a while, rather than saying anything, so she continued. "Whoever Artie Ingram contacted put him in touch with you. You organized a meeting, and you offered to pay Ingram for the vials of Ebola. Ingram agreed to ten million pounds. He stole the vials and killed his girlfriend, who had agreed to help him into the hospital as she was feeling bitter about not being accepted into medical school. So now Artie had the vials of Ebola. However, for the second part of the plan, he needed help. He needed someone local. He reached out to Petkovic, a dual citizen of both Serbia and England, who lives here full-time and knows the city. However, Petkovic betrayed Ingram and shot him, stealing the vials. Are you with me still?"

"This story is insane. It's the fabrication of a crazy person," Roman said. Still, I could see a thin sheen of sweat on his forehead. Violet was definitely getting to him.

"Ingram had left your details on his fridge. After killing him, Petkovic called you, and you agreed to allow him to continue the plan, and pay him instead.

The attack is supposed to happen today; that much I know. I suspect that if one were to look at your recent trades, you would have made a number of short sales today, in anticipation of the attack. You must be banking on quite the payday in order to pay ten million to some gangsters. Unfortunately for you, Petkovic and his second-in-command are in prison. However, fortunately for you, there is still time to make a deal. As you can see, I know everything. Everything except where the attack will be taking place. If you help me, I can help you."

"You have no proof of any of this," Anthony Roman replied. "If you did, you'd simply arrest me."

"Ah, *mais tu vois*, I am not with the police. I do not care about arresting people; I care about finding the Ebola. I can ensure, however, that you will have the opportunity to make an advantageous deal with the Crown Prosecutor should Cassie and I find the Ebola vials before they are unleashed on the general public. I have figured all of this out without needing any proof. How long do you think it will take me to find proof of all of this once I actually begin to look for it? You are now betting your freedom on my own stupidity. Trust me, you will lose."

At this point, Anthony Roman was visibly sweating, and looking around for an exit. Violet almost had him; I was sure of it. "Your job involves taking calculated risk. Do not bet against me," she told him. "Tell me where the Ebola is supposed to be released."

She stared Anthony Roman down for another thirty seconds or so, and finally, he broke down.

"I don't know," he finally said. "I honestly don't know where the attack is going to be. All I know is that through one of their guys, named Sasha or something, they'll be able to access somewhere where they can spread the virus as efficiently as possible."

"Sasha. Is that all you know?"

Anthony Roman nodded miserably. "Look, what kind of deal do you think I can get?"

"I think it will depend on whether or not Cassie and I manage to find the Ebola vials in time. Move," she said, plugging the powerboard back in and getting up and making her way to where Roman was sitting. He got up off his chair and Violet began tapping away at his computer. She tossed me her phone.

"Text DCI Williams that we are ready," she told me, and I did as she asked. About two minutes later the man himself came up the stairs, followed closely by two other detectives.

"Anthony Roman, you are under arrest at this time," DCI Williams told him, and Roman sighed as he turned around and put his hands behind his back. Evidently all the fight had gone out of him after realizing just how much Violet knew. "You do not have to say anything but it may harm your defense if you do not mention, when questioned, something which you later rely on in court. Anything you do say may be given in evidence."

He handed Roman off to the other two men, who left the room, one flanking Roman on each side, and DCI Williams turned to me while Violet typed away on the man's computer.

"Are you any closer to finding the virus?" he asked. I shrugged.

"Well, we know the attack is going to be today, and we know it's one of the men in the Serbian gang named Sasha who's the main player now. The rest is up to her," I said, motioning to Violet.

"It is always up to me, and I am always correct. Come, we must go immediately. It is already after four thirty. If I estimate correctly, the attack will take place sometime before six tonight. Possibly as early as five o'clock."

"Where are we going?" DCI Williams asked as the three of us practically sprinted out the door.

"Waterloo Station!" Violet called behind her.

My heart clenched when I heard the words. Waterloo Station was the busiest train station in London, and one of the busiest in the world. I was pretty sure I'd read in one of my guide books a few months ago that around one hundred million people traveled via Waterloo every year, meaning there could be as many as three hundred thousand passengers passing through in a day. I knew for a fact that at rush hour, the place was always jam packed with people leaving work and heading back home.

"I have a car parked outside," DCI Williams said, panting slightly, as the elevator made its way down the shaft. What had felt like such a high-speed adventure the first time I'd taken it now felt like a snail's pace. We had to get to Waterloo Station.

"No," Violet said. "The tube will be much faster."

Normally, the fact that I'd had an ACL reconstruction–combined with the fact that my regular exercise schedule was non-existent–meant that I wouldn't be able to keep up with Violet and DCI Williams as we ran down Leadenhall Street toward Bank Underground station. However, this time, adrenaline coursed through my veins and if there was a protest from my knee, my brain ignored it. We only had a few minutes left to stop a terrorist attack, after all.

I really, really hoped we were going to make it in time.

CHAPTER 21

*W*hen we reached the fare gates at Bank Station, Violet didn't even bother tapping in; she simply jumped onto the panel where you tapped your Oyster card, then jumped over the paddle gate. DCI Williams already had his Oyster card out, and mine was in my back pocket, so I grabbed it and the two of us scanned in. A transit police officer was yelling at Violet, but DCI Williams flashed his badge and yelled "it's ok, she's with me," at the man, who backed down. We followed Violet as we raced through a veritable labyrinth of one-way tunnels, escalators and sloping tunnels toward the platform for the Waterloo and City line headed to Waterloo, and immediately jumped onto a waiting train. I'd never been so thankful to make a train in my life.

My heart pounded in my chest. I knew the ride

would take around four minutes–Waterloo was only two stations away–and I also knew they were going to be the longest four minutes of my life. Violet, on the other hand, seemed as calm as if we were just going down to the pub for a drink.

"Tell me, Cassie," Violet told me. "If the virus was released into the air, what would happen?"

I thought back to what I'd learned about Ebola. "Well, honestly, nothing really. Ebola isn't like the flu. It's not an airborne disease. If someone infected with Ebola sneezed in your face, and droplets of their saliva got into your mouth or nose, you would be infected via the air, but technically it would be from the droplets of saliva."

"So the HVAC system is unlikely to be the target. It is bodily fluids only, yes?"

"Exactly," I said. "Blood is the best carrier of the virus, if I remember right. One milliliter of blood can carry one million particles of the disease."

"Fluids," Violet said quietly, almost to herself. "How do you get every person passing through Waterloo station to be covered in fluids?"

I had no idea. After all, it wasn't like every single person used the bathroom. Suddenly, Violet perked up.

"The sprinkler system!" she exclaimed. "It has to be. Cassie, how would it work?"

I thought for a few moments. "Well, if they injected the virus into some blood, the virus would thrive there. However, as soon as the blood was added to regular tap water, the virus would be killed within minutes. Because the tap water doesn't have the same salt concentration as our blood, water would rush into the blood cells to even out the salt concentration, making them burst and killing the virus. Assuming they put the blood in regular tap water, the sprinklers would have to be set off within about one minute or else the virus would be useless."

"Well, we can always hope these guys are idiots," DCI Williams muttered. "But let's try and stop this all the same."

"Agreed," Violet said, nodding. The lady announced that we were at Waterloo Station, and we piled to the front of the line. As soon as the doors opened the three of us practically burst out of them. I followed Violet blindly as she expertly navigated the corridors, and within a minute we found ourselves standing in the center of Waterloo Station, a hub of activity.

The air buzzed with the hum of people talking, be it on their phones or to each other. Men in suits carrying briefcases rushed by while tourists stood in front of the departures board trying to find their platforms. Students carrying backpacks that weighed more than most children walked past giggling, and smartly dressed businesswomen closed deals on their phones.

As soon as we walked in, however, I focused on

the roof. The semi-transparent tiles let the light in, giving the whole area an airy feel. The rectangular panes and criss-crossed steel beams made the building feel like it was built during the Industrial Revolution. Speakerphones hung down from the ceiling, but more importantly, if I looked very closely, I could see sprinklers on every few beams.

"We have to find out how to get to the sprinkler system," DCI Williams said. "I can ask someone."

"There is no need," Violet said as she made her way toward the room to buy tickets. "I already know where to go." At the entrance was a large orange door announcing 'Keep Clear–Emergency Exit Only'. To the left of that door, however, was another, this one just plain brown. Violet made a move to open it, but it was locked. Cursing, she grabbed her lock picking tools from her purse and thirty seconds later the door was opened.

We entered and found ourselves at the entrance of a stairwell, one of those crappy cement ones that literally every building on the planet seems to have somewhere. Taking the steps three at a time, Violet and DCI Williams bounded upwards, while I ran up as best I could. Going up stairs didn't hurt anymore, but I still wasn't able to take them two at a time.

When we reached the top of the stairs, another door led us into a hallway. We passed multiple rooms, none of which were labeled, but Violet seemed to know exactly where she was going.

"How do you know where the sprinkler room in Waterloo Station is?" DCI Williams asked, wheezing slightly.

"I live in London, I make it my business to know every corner of this city," Violet replied.

"There's a difference between knowing where to get your kale smoothies and being able to navigate the back rooms of a major train station though," I said, laughing through my gasps as my lungs sucked in air.

"And that difference means we might be able to stop a terrorist attack today," Violet said.

"Point taken," I replied as Violet slowed up. We stopped in front of a plain, beige-colored door. Unfortunately, this one was padlocked.

"I knew I should not have left my stethoscope at home," Violet muttered. "This one will take me a moment," she said.

"I have a better idea," DCI Williams said, moving to a fire extinguisher hanging on the wall about twenty feet away. He grabbed it and made his way back to the door, bashing the lock and breaking it on the third attempt.

"Your method has not the finesse of mine, but I cannot deny its effectiveness," Violet said. Suddenly, she stopped short.

"Wait," she said, crouching down to the ground. There was some white powder on the ground. For what felt like the hundredth time today, my heart seized in my chest. White powder on the ground near a water supply we were fairly certain terrorists were about to use? This was not good. DCI Williams and I shared a look of worry, but Violet simply picked up some of the powder and put it in her mouth.

"Are you insane?" I practically shrieked at her. "Why would you do that?"

"Relax, it was nothing more than regular table salt," Violet told me with a smile. "If it was anthrax, we would likely have already been infected anyway."

"Oh so that makes it ok to eat the random powder off the ground then."

"What it does tell us is that the Serbians have been doing their research. If they have added salt to the water supply and then added blood to which the Ebola was introduced, the virus will last for longer inside the sprinkler system."

"That's it," DCI Williams said. "That's all I needed to see. I'm putting out an order to evacuate the station."

"It is a good idea, that one," Violet said, nodding, as the three of us made our way into the room. "However, make sure that your evacuation is subtle. We do not want to spook the man into bringing his timetable forward." DCI Williams nodded and pulled out his phone and then went back out into the hallway to make a call while Violet and I stood in what was evidently the main fire safety room for the whole station.

In the center of the room was a large, black box labeled 'Sprinklers'. Violet and I made our way toward it, and a few seconds later I'd realized how it works.

"The water comes from there," I said, motioning toward a large pipe entering the room with a cut-off valve set to 'off'. No water was coming in. From there, the water entered the storage and was pushed out via another pipe that left the room from the other side. This one had a cut-off valve as well, but someone had broken it so that without a wrench it would be impossible to turn off the water flow.

Violet had been right. This was where the attack was happening.

"Sasha Bakic works at Waterloo Station," Violet told me. "His shift this morning began at five, hence the moving of the vials. He would not have had time during his shift, especially during the rush hour, to infect the water, so he has had to wait until afterwards. His shift ended at three this afternoon. He has prepared the tank; there is more salt inside the water. He will likely bring blood contaminated with Ebola in here soon and add it to the sprinkler system, then override the computer here to set off the sprinklers."

"Therefore covering everyone in the station with an Ebola infected blood and water mixture, hoping that some of it gets into their eyes, their mouths or even just a cut on their skin, and infects them," I finished.

"*Oui*, that is the plan."

"All so one guy could make some money on his stocks," I said, shaking my head.

"There is a lot of money in it. When London was attacked in 2007, I remember the story of one broker who made hundreds of millions of pounds. He had no pre-knowledge of the attacks; he simply bought travel stocks when the markets dropped immediately after the attacks, and made the money on the rebound afterwards."

"So how do we stop this?" I asked, looking at the computer.

"You are looking in the wrong spot," Violet said, suddenly making her way toward the large black box. It was about three feet high, and she jumped on top of it with ease. "Yes," she said, nodding. "This is the true problem."

I moved over to where Violet was and gasped. I hadn't noticed it before, but a small hole had been opened on top of the sprinkler system's water storage unit; it would have been designed for easy testing of the water inside the sprinkler system. On top of the hole was a shoebox, with a cell phone with a number of different colored cables protruding from it taped to the side. There was about a pint of blood at the bottom of the box.

"Is that… a bomb?" I asked, my eyebrows coming closer together as I frowned at the box.

Violet nodded. "Of sorts. It is not a bomb with

explosives, however. The box contains the Ebola-infected blood. When Bakic calls the number associated with the cell phone, it will send a small charge of electricity through the edge of the box, will be strong enough to make a hole in the cardboard. The bottom will fall away, and the blood will enter the sprinkler's water supply. We must diffuse the cell phone charge before Bakic makes that phone call," she said. "The bottom of the box has been glued securely to the water sprinkler system, so attempting to remove it will tear the cardboard and again, the blood will enter the water system."

"Please tell me you know how to diffuse a bomb."

"It is like you barely know me at all. Of course I know how to diffuse a bomb like this. The easiest way would be to stick a paperclip into the side of the phone and remove the SIM card, deactivating the phone, but he has thought of that. There is a sheet of metal over the slot. No, I have to figure out the charge and cut one of the cables. Cassie, at the computer in the far corner of the room is some of the security camera footage from the ground floor. Could you please tell me how the evacuation is going?"

I went to where Violet instructed me to, trying to keep calm. We were in a room with a bomb. Not one that was going to blow us up, but one that could kill a whole bunch of people all the same. I looked at the screen. There was a much larger police presence than before, and people seemed to be acting in a relatively orderly manner, but they were filing out of the station incredibly slowly. And then, just to make matters worse, a train pulled up to one of the platforms and people began piling out. Apparently the order to evacuate the station hadn't included stopping all the trains.

"I don't want to say bad things about DCI Williams, but umm, I really hope you do know what you're doing," I told Violet.

"Is it obvious they are evacuating?"

"Yes."

"Sometimes I do not know why I even bother. I told DCI Williams to be subtle about it. Now as soon as Bakic notices, he will set off the charge. We likely have under two minutes."

Violet reached into her purse and took out a pair of latex gloves and slipped them on, then grabbed a Swiss Army Knife and placed it next to her.

"Wait," I said. "Are you putting your hands in blood we know has been infected with Ebola?"

"I need to see the other end of the cables in order to be able to cut the correct cable, and there is no way to do that without moving the blood around. Stand back, Cassie, and do not worry. After all, I am wearing gloves."

I took a step back as Violet began stirring the blood around, trying to see the bottom of the box. I knew she was being careful, and then suddenly, I glanced at the security cameras again. In the corner of the building people were rushing toward a growing wave of smoke.

"Uhhh, Violet, I think Bakic just set his fire, you're out of time. Pick a wire and cut it."

Violet smiled at me as she grabbed the knife, took one of the green cables and cut it. I looked into the box. The blood was still there; it wasn't leaking into the water system. She hadn't cut the wrong cord.

Ten seconds later, the phone began to ring. Violet and I looked at each other, and Violet smiled. I looked down into the box. Still no leakage. I began to laugh. We had done it!

Ok, 'we' was a strong word. I was well aware that Violet had done almost everything, but still! I was here. I had seen it all happen.

"I told you I knew how to diffuse a bomb," Violet told me. "I cannot believe you thought I would fail against a gangster who looked up how to make a cell phone bomb on the internet. Now, let us text DCI Williams that despite his best efforts, the terrorist attack has been averted."

Just then, the water storage system roared to life. The mechanical sound of the pump inside sending water to the sprinkler system made me jump about a foot in the air, until I realized what was happening. Bakic's smoke had worked; the sprinkler system was set off.

Fortunately, however, the contaminated blood

was still in the cardboard box on top of the water system, and not inside it. About three minutes later all the water inside the storage system had been pumped out.

We had done it. We had stopped the Ebola attack on London. Everyone was safe now. Violet pulled out her phone and sent a text quickly.

Two minutes later DCI Williams entered the room. He was soaking wet, his hair plastered to his forehead.

"You couldn't have stopped the sprinkler system working completely, could you?" he asked with a grin on his face before rushing forward and taking Violet into a big bear hug. I grinned as she squealed.

"You are soaking wet! What kind of man hugs a woman when he looks like a half-drowned bear! If this is how you repay me I will never stop another terrorist attack for you ever again!"

DCI Williams and I laughed as he let Violet go and she flipped him the bird. It was all over. I was so happy I felt like I was floating.

CHAPTER 22

*O*ver the next few hours we began to understand everything that had happened.

As soon as DCI Williams came up he apologized. "I honestly did try to make the evacuation as subtle as possible. Unfortunately, as soon as everyone realized what was going on, they all formed an orderly queue to leave the station, which made what we were doing incredibly obvious."

I hid my smile at those words; since moving to London I'd learned that the British really love their line-ups, or queues as they call them. In America everyone would have run toward the doors in a mad rush to be the first ones out; here everyone lined up in an orderly manner and awaited their turn patiently. It was just all too civilized.

Sasha Bakic had been arrested; as soon as DCI Williams saw the smoke he knew what the man was trying to do. He arrested Bakic, but not before enough smoke had been generated to trigger the sprinkler system. About two hundred people still left inside the train station had been sprayed with the water, and while they were all upset, at least none of them had any risk of being infected with Ebola.

The police managed to keep the details out of the press as well, although it was leaked that the police did stop a potential terrorist attack. For the next few weeks, at least, the Metropolitan Police were considered heroes, and at one point Violet told me she heard from "her sources" that DCI Williams was being considered for a promotion.

Sasha Bakic, Filip Petkovic and Dragan all admitted to everything once their lawyers learned what kind of evidence we had against them. Violet and I were allowed to observe as DCI Williams took their statements before they made their agreements with the Crown Prosecutor. They had all agreed to deals that would involve them spending the next forty years of their lives in prison. The pizza shop around the corner from Dragan's home had definitely lost a regular customer.

"Is this the first terrorist attack you've stopped?" I asked Violet as we watched DCI Williams asking Petkovic questions about how he came into contact with Anthony Roman.

"No," Violet replied. "It is, however, the most creative, and certainly the one that came closest to succeeding. However, you say that I am the one who stopped it. You are technically incorrect. It was just as much you as it was I."

"Who are you and what have you done with Violet?" I asked. "Not only are you being humble, but you're also wrong. You figured the whole thing out. I'd still be staring at the hospital camera footage, wondering who the man who killed Anita Turner was if it was all up to me."

Violet gave me one of those small smiles of hers. "I am not often humble, but I cannot deny the facts. It is true. Had you not come to my home, and had you not made the comment about terrorist attacks not occurring due to money, I would not have realized that you were wrong, discovered the true motive, and we would not have found Sasha Bakic in time."

"There are nicer ways to phrase that than 'you were so wrong I figured out the answer,'" I replied with a smile.

"There are, but they would be less correct. You were instrumental in solving this case. Do not discount your contribution because I was the one who cut the wire. Without you, we never would have found the wire to cut. There is a reason I ask you to some of my crime scenes. I have found it advantageous to speak with another human being about crimes, and most people do not like me enough to have long conversations about them with me."

I grinned. "Gee, I wonder why that is."

"It is because I am blunt. But I can be, because I am very good at what I do. I am glad you were here with me on this case, Cassie. Without you, the attack would have undoubtedly succeeded."

"Thanks," I replied, a small blush starting to creep up my neck. I had never really considered myself as having an important role in any of Violet's investigations. I was more of a tag-along in my head; the person who watched the adventure unfold while not really being a part of it. Violet–especially Violet, who didn't have a single humble bone in her body–telling me that I was a major reason why a terrorist attack had been avoided made me feel like I had done something good for the world.

And the warm, fuzzy feeling it gave me was something I would cherish forever.

"You see? When you drink a smoothie, with actual vitamins and minerals, good things happen," Violet joked, and I punched her in the arm.

"The smoothie was a coincidence," I retorted, and she laughed.

* * *

TWO DAYS later I was sitting on the couch with my iPad, nestled in the crook of Jake's arm. Biscuit was sitting on his lap, purring.

"He's my boyfriend, you know," I told my cat,

glaring at Biscuit as he demanded more attention from Jake than I did. Jake laughed.

"Are you sure you want to do this?" he asked, looking at the screen.

I nodded. "Yes. I don't have to do anything with it right away, but Brianne is right. This way the option is there if I need it."

I clicked the submit button, and a minute later a confirmation popped up on my screen. My transcript, with every class I'd ever taken at Stanford, along with the record of my residency, was going to be printed out, signed by an authority at the University and mailed to me here in England.

A warm glow passed through me. I was happy I'd ordered my transcript. When it arrived, I was going to apply to medical school.

"I now have a few weeks to decide what specialty I want to apply for," I told Jake.

"Well, I think pathology, but of course I'm biased. But pathology is where all the sexy people go, so it's where you belong," he told me, leaning down and planting a kiss on my lips.

I smiled at him. "Well you're living proof of that being true."

"Could you tell I was fishing for the compliment?"

"Just a little," I smiled. "I'm thinking of maybe going into immunology. There wouldn't really be much of a surgical requirement, and I like the idea of studying germs."

"Sounds good," Jake said. "Whatever you decide, I'm all for it. Although from what I hear, you're pretty good at hunting terrorists, too."

"What do you mean, from what you hear? I was going to wait until we go out to tell you all about it."

"Violet came down to the morgue today."

"Does she have another case?" I asked, and I noticed my stomach sinking into my stomach just a little bit. I had to admit it; the thought of Violet not asking me to join her in her cases made me a little bit sad, especially after her speech to me in the police station the day before.

"No," Jake shook his head. "Whenever Violet has nothing to do she comes down to the morgue to look for interesting murder cases, or to watch autopsies, or to try and convince me to let her do experiments on the bodies."

I laughed. "That does sound exactly like something she would do. Do you let her?"

Jake shook his head. "Usually not. If the person was an organ donor, or decided to give their body to science, I let her do it. For the organ donors, however, I only let her do experiments on the organs that would have otherwise been discarded for whatever reason."

"What does she do with them?" I asked. "A part of me doesn't want to know, but my morbid curiosity really wants to."

Jake laughed. "Usually she just tests how long it

takes for bruises to appear, and what shapes bruises take when the skin is hit with various instruments. I've seen her do some chemical tests on other organs though. I'm really not sure. But she came in yesterday. I didn't have any bodies for her to work on, so she just watched me do an autopsy. She told me you were instrumental in stopping that terrorist attack."

Once again I felt the blush crawl up my face. "She's exaggerating," I replied. "I honestly didn't really do much."

"If there's one thing Violet Despuis doesn't do, it's exaggerate. I'm really proud of you. You got into a situation most people would have balked at, and you ended up being one of the reasons why the terrorist threat alert got dropped today."

"Thanks," I told Jake, nestling into him further. "It's kind of you to say."

"Now I want details!" he said. "What's the point of dating the woman who just saved all of London if she won't even tell you exactly how it all happened?"

I laughed. "All right, all right," I said. "But you're buying dinner."

"Deal," Jake grinned. Biscuit meowed in appreciation.

"I think his vote is that we get chicken," I said as Jake stroked his orange fur.

As I got up and went to the kitchen to open a bottle of wine while Jake grabbed my tablet to order something from JustEat, I realized that for the first time in a long, long time, I was absolutely, perfectly content. I didn't know where my life was going to go in the future. But I was going to do something with my life. I had the perfect boyfriend, friends who cared about me, and over the last week or so I'd actually made a difference in the world.

Yup, things were definitely looking up. I couldn't wait to see where life was going to take me next.

BOOK 4: Cassie's adventures continue in Strangled in Soho. When a woman is found strangled in the London borough of Soho, the police think it's a suicide, but Violet Despuis knows better, and Cassie knows that if Violet thinks it's murder, it's murder. Now they just need to prove it.

Click or tap here to read Strangled in Soho now.

Thank you so much for reading! If you enjoyed Whacked in Whitechapel please help other readers find this book so they can enjoy it, too.

- Write a review on Amazon
- Sign up for my newsletter here to be the first to find out about new releases: http://www.samanthasilverwrites.com/newsletter
- Check out the next book in this series, Bombing in Belgravia, by clicking here: http://www.samanthasilverwrites.com/strangledinsoho

You can also check out any of the other series I write by clicking the links below:

Non-Paranormal Cozy Mysteries

Cassie Coburn Mysteries

Ruby Bay Mysteries

Paranormal Cozy Mysteries

Western Woods Mysteries

Pacific North Witches Mysteries

Pacific Cove Mysteries

Willow Bay Witches Mysteries

Magical Bookshop Mysteries

California Witching Mysteries

ABOUT THE AUTHOR

Samantha Silver lives in British Columbia, Canada, along with her husband and a little old doggie named Terra. She loves animals, skiing and of course, writing cozy mysteries.

You can connect with Samantha online here:
Facebook
Email

Made in United States
Orlando, FL
03 January 2024

42011410R00125